Sunflowers and Second Chances

BY:

ANNA POE

Copyright Notice

Sunflowers and Second Chances

© 2026 by Anna Poe

Published by Anna Poe
P.O. Box 4452, Winchester, KY 40392-4452
www.annapoe.com

Names: Poe, Anna, author.

[ ]p. 5 in. × 8 in. (12.70 cm × 20.32 cm)

Description: Anna Poe digital eBook edition | Anna Poe Trade paperback edition | Winchester, KY: Anna Poe, 2026.

Library of Congress Cataloging-in-Publication Data

Names: Poe, Anna, author.

Title: Sunflowers and Second Chances / Anna Poe

Summary: In the golden fields of a Kentucky sunflower farm, big-city marketer Lila Harper rediscovers small-town roots and a second chance at love with her protective ex, Jake Bradford, as they fight developers threatening their shared legacy.

Identifiers: ePCN: [pending] | ISBN-13: 978-1-68190-313-2 (trade) |

1. clean contemporary romance fiction 2. Second chance romance 3. small-town Kentucky romance 4. City girl country boy 5. Hometown return romance 6. Saving the family farm 7. sweet closed-door romance

Subjects: LCSH: Farm life—Kentucky—Fiction. | Homecoming—Fiction. | Man-woman relationships—Fiction. | LCGFT: Romance fiction. | Domestic fiction. | Pastoral fiction.

Chapter 1

Lila Harper steered the new signing through the rooftop crowd with one hand at the girl's back and the other holding a champagne flute she had not touched.

The city glittered below them, restless and bright. Drinks flowed freely and people laughed too loud. Cassidy Park, the new launch, tried very hard to look like she belonged.

"Two more pictures," Lila said, easing the girl forward. "Then we hand you off to the radio guy. Then you breathe."

"I'm breathing."

"You're holding it. Different thing entirely."

Cassidy laughed, and her shoulders came down a half inch. Lila kept her hand at the small of the girl's back and aimed her at the photographer, who had been waiting forty-five minutes for a clean shot and was about to abandon his post for a third drink.

"Smile like you've already won," Lila said.

"I haven't."

"Tonight you have. That's the whole job."

Cassidy smiled. The flash went off twice, and the photographer signaled across the crowd that he was satisfied for once. Katy caught Lila's eye from the far side of the rooftop and gave her the half-nod that meant good, keep going.

Lila kept going. The label held a launch every six weeks, sometimes more often. Her weeks ran on a rhythm she could set a watch by. Marketing director was a job description that fit on a business card. The job itself entailed holding a hundred details and never dropping the champagne.

She handed Cassidy off to the radio guy with a quiet word of warning about which questions the girl might freeze on, and stepped back to scan for the next person who needed her hand at a back.

A man from the promotions desk waved her over. He had the look of somebody about to ask for something he wasn't sure he could ask for, and Lila reached him before he was ready, which was the simplest method.

"Tell me," she said.

"Cassidy on a Tuesday morning at six? With Casey? Because Casey owes me, and I want to use it on her before she remembers."

"Tuesday at six. Done."

"You don't have to ask Katy?"

"I just did. You watched me. She nodded. Tuesday at six."

He laughed, clearly relieved. "Bless you, Harper."

"Don't bless me yet. The girl'll need coffee and somebody to walk her into the studio."

She turned back into the crowd, and the angle of a denim jacket she had not stopped recognizing caught at the corner of her eye. Cole Banks stood at the far rail with his elbow on the marble and a beer in his hand, talking to a redhead Lila did not know. He had not looked over yet, and she did not let him.

There had been a night two years ago when she had finally finished a fight with him without raising her voice, and she had walked out of his apartment and decided in that minute to never raise her voice for him again. She had nearly kept the promise.

She crossed away from the rail and put a high-top between herself and his sightline.

Lila set the untouched flute on a nearby high-top and checked her phone out of habit. Then she scanned the crowd for the next person who needed something.

"You look like a girl who could use a drink," Katy said at her elbow. She set a glass of red wine in front of Lila with a small ceremony.

"Not while I'm working."

"It's a launch, Lila. You can drink at your own launches." Katy lifted her perfectly frosted hair off her neck in deference to the Nashville July heat.

"I don't drink at the ones with this many phones in the room."

Katy snorted. "You drink at none of them." She looked her up and down, from the top of her blonde hair over the loose white dress that brushed her mid-thigh, to the toes of her white boots. "I never would have put you in an all-white outfit. I would have thought it would wash you out. Wow, you knocked it out of the park."

Her cheeks went hot. "Thanks, friend."

They watched the room together for a beat. Katy gave Lila her first real job seven years ago. She'd walked into the Starboard interview in the only blazer she owned, saying things she'd practiced on the four-hour drive, and Katy hired her on the spot.

"Cassidy's good," Katy said.

"She is."

"The press kit was brilliant. Well done."

Lila knew it was. "Thanks." She watched Cassidy accept a glass of water. "This town is going to eat her up and spit her out."

Katy tapped her turquoise necklace with her manicured nail. "It often does. We'll see what she looks like on the other side."

Lila laughed. The sound came out dry.

Her phone buzzed against the high-top.

She glanced at it on instinct, expecting the Casey radio booking confirmation. The screen said Charlie Bradford instead.

She went still.

Charlie did not call. He had texted her exactly twice in eleven years, both times to confirm a Christmas package address. The last time Lila had seen Charlie Bradford in person had been at his parents' funeral eleven years ago.

Something was wrong. *Please don't let it be Jake.* She hit the green button and turned her shoulder to the launch.

"Charlie?"

"Lila." His voice had the same flatness Jake's voice had always had. "Hey. So. Mae had a heart attack."

All of the noise around her disappeared.

"How bad?"

"Mild. They told me to use that word, mild, six different times. She's at the hospital in Lexington, and they're keeping her overnight for sure, probably tomorrow as well. The doctor said stable."

"When?"

"This afternoon. Jake found her in the kitchen. She was conscious but couldn't get to the phone."

Lila watched a drop of condensation slide down the champagne flute. "I'll be there." Should she fly or drive? Drive. She should drive. "I'm leaving right now."

"Drive careful."

"Charlie." She kept her voice steady. "Tell her I'm coming."

"I'll tell her."

Lila stood with the phone against her ear for a full beat after the line had gone dead.

Katy narrowed her eyes and watched her. Finally, she asked, "Your grandma?"

Lila nodded once. "Go," Katy said.

"Cassidy still has the radio piece. And the seven a.m. with Country Now, and the meeting with—"

"Lila."

"And Wednesday I have a—"

"Lila, go."

⟨———🐝——∞——🐞———⟩

Lila got to her apartment in twenty-two minutes flat. She changed into jeans and boots and left five minutes later, a suitcase haphazardly packed.

By eleven-fifteen she was on I-65 north. Thankfully, traffic was thin this time of night. She drove with both hands at ten and two and the radio off while she thought about Mae.

She'd never known her parents. Her mother left her with Mae when she was six months old and just never came back. Mae had taught her to drive on a tractor and pull the cultivator when she was eleven. She taught her how to bundle sunflowers for their booth at Fox Hollow's Fall Kickoff Festival when she was twelve. She sewed her prom dress, took a thousand pictures at her graduation, and sent her care packages once a month in college.

Mae did not have heart attacks. Mae was supposed to outlive them all.

As she entered Bowling Green her gas light came on. She got off of the exit and pulled into the closest gas station. As she turned her car off, she just sat there for a moment and suddenly tears filled her eyes. She didn't know what she would do if Mae wasn't there anymore. Her breath hiccupped and she pressed her fingers to her eyes. She still wore the stupid fake lashes from the kickoff event.

She breathed in and out slowly. As soon as she felt some control return, she dabbed under her eyes to make sure the makeup stayed in place, then got out to pump the gas.

She drove east and got to Lexington just as the sky began to lighten. It took no time to find a parking space in the hospital's garage. She checked her phone and found the text from Charlie that gave her the room number. In the elevator, she checked her reflection in the elevator doors. Her hair had started to come out of her braid and her eyeliner had smeared a little. She wiped under her eyes, took a deep breath, and stepped out of the elevator.

Mae was smaller than she had been at Christmas.

Lila stood in the doorway of the room and kept her hand on the frame for a beat, just to steady the tilt of the world. Her precious grandmother wore a hospital gown, hooked to to two leads and an IV. She wore her glasses and looked up from her book when she heard Lila at the door. Immediately, a smile covered her face.

"Lila Grace."

"Hi, Granny Mae."

She held out her thin arms. "Get over here."

Lila crossed the room and let Mae pull her close. She didn't smell like lilacs like she had her entire life. She would go home and get her lotion so she could smell right.

"You didn't need to come," Mae said as she release her.

"Don't be silly." She sat down in the orange chair beside the bed and took Mae's hand. "You scared me."

"I scared myself."

"They said mild," Lila said.

"They said mild a lot. I don't think the word changed anything in the actual ventricle."

Mae was still Mae. "That sounds like a Mae sentence."

"I'm tired but I'm me." She reached over and patted her hand. "Did Jake call you?"

Lila's heart gave a little tug. She shook her head. "Charlie."

"He's a good boy."

She thought Charlie would likely take exception to being called a boy by anyone but Mae. "Jake found me. They let him ride in the ambulance with me."

"I'm glad he was there."

"He was here until he had to go do the evening milking. I imagine he'll be back soon."

Lila looked at the door as if Mae had conjured Jake. She licked her lips. "Can I get you anything?"

"No, Sugar." She closed her eyes. "I'll just rest now that I know you got here safe." After a second, she opened them again. "I have things to discuss with you," she said, her voice slurry with tired.

"There's time," Lila whispered. As Mae fell asleep, Lila lay her head on bed next to their clasped hands and closed her eyes. A tear slid over the bridge of her nose and plopped onto the sheet.

<——∞——>

Jake Bradford pushed the door open with the back of his hand and stepped into the room.

He had expected to see two heads on the way in. Mae's silver, on the high pillow. Lila's auburn, on the orange chair beside the bed.

The chair was empty.

His jaw tightened slightly. He did not say anything yet.

"There he is," Mae said. She set her book face-down on her chest and shifted her glasses.

"Morning, Granny Mae." She was not his grandmother, but all of his life he'd called her that and it never felt right to stop.

"Get over here. Don't stand in the doorway."

He walked over and bent and kissed the top of her head. Then stepped back.

"How was the milking?"

"Fine."

He sat down in the orange chair and examined Mae. He'd come over to see if she needed him to mow her lawn and found her on the kitchen floor. She'd scared him. He didn't mind admitting that.

Mae had picked up her book again and watched him quietly over the top of it.

"What?"

"Spit it out, son."

"Nothing to spit."

"You're holding that cap like you're about to break the brim."

He forced his hands to relax. "I just expected she'd be here."

Mae let her book fall flat to her chest. "Lila Grace went home about two hours ago. She was going to shower, eat something, and feed the cat. Said she'd be back about lunch."

He did not say anything right away. His chest loosened. He hadn't known he was braced.

"All right."

"All right."

"No cat ever died missing a meal. Especially that one." He was intentionally trying to lighten up the conversation.

"Sugar, that cat would have starved for a week and Lila wouldn't put it on a person's conscience."

He nearly laughed.

Mae lifted her hand from her book and patted the rail of the bed. "You don't have to sit here."

"You don't have to try to tell me what to do."

She gave a small, "Hmph." Then picked her book back up. After a moment, she set it down again. "Jake."

"Yes, ma'am?"

"She didn't put your mama and daddy in that plane." His hands went cold. "She's not the reason you didn't leave."

He stared at her for a long time. Emotion churned in his stomach. Finally, he said, "She didn't come home that first harvest you brought in alone." He paused. "She didn't ever come home."

"No. I don't begrudge her finding a life, Jacob Michael. You shouldn't, either."

He knew that. But he'd hoped that after college, since he couldn't come to her, she'd choose to come to him. And...well, that was a long time ago.

He thought about the magazine on Charlie's counter at the Feed and Seed last August. The cover with Lila on it in some white dress with her hair all fancy and curled with her arm at the shoulder of the country singer with the deliberately torn jeans. Suddenly, he'd known she would never return.

Had he been waiting all this time?

Mae settled her hand on top of his. "You know what I think, son?"

"What?"

"I think you've been carrying her for a long time and you don't know how to put her down."

He let out a long sigh and looked at the clock above the door. Twenty minutes to noon. Lila had told Mae she would be back about lunch. As much as he'd prepared himself since last night to see her, he suddenly couldn't do it.

He stood. "I'll let you rest," he said.

"Hmmm." She kept her eyes closed. He bent and kissed her silver hair then walked out the door. He didn't relax again until he slid into his truck cab without encountering Miss Lila Harper from Nashville, Tennessee who finally deigned to return.

Chapter 2

Lila lifted Mae's overnight bag out of the bed of the truck and set it on the gravel beside the running board.

The heat rose up from the gravel drive. The Kentucky July offered little relief from the streak of hundred degree days. Cicadas pulsed steadily in the trees by the lane. Lila pushed her sunglasses up into her hair and walked slowly around the front of the truck.

Mae had the door already half open. She had refused a wheelchair at discharge. Really, she'd refused everything except the brown paper bag of medications wedged in her elbow.

"Let me help you," Lila said.

"I've got me, Sugar."

"I know you do." Lila held out her hand anyway. "Take it for me, then. So I feel useful."

Mae's mouth ticked slightly at one corner. She put a thin hand in Lila's. Lila steadied her down to the gravel. Two days in a hospital bed left her ankles uncertain. Mae set both boots flat. She stood for a beat, looking up at her own house as if she had been gone a year.

"Well," Mae said. "Still here."

"Of course it's still here."

"I haven't slept away from here for a decade or more. Wasn't sure it would stay if I was gone."

Lila kept her face carefully neutral and tucked Mae's bag under her arm. "You're not climbing those stairs until I see you eat something."

"I ain't never seen oatmeal quite that shade of gray."

"I'll make you something fresh."

They walked together to the bottom of the porch steps. Mae stopped to catch her breath. One hand on the railing. The other at her own collarbone, like she was checking the wiring. Lila stood at her shoulder and made herself breathe slowly alongside her.

She looked past Mae, out across the yard.

The Harper sunflowers should have been a wall by July, six and seven feet tall, their faces all turned the same direction, a yellow press from the road to the equipment shed. Lila had grown up walking the rows with twine in her back pocket. She had bundled for Mae's booth since she was tall enough to handle the shears.

This year there were gaps.

Whole stretches of bare ground showed between the rows. Where the wall should have been was a thin and uneven scatter. What plants remained stood stunted and leaning, with bald gaps where whole clusters had failed. The baler sat in the side yard, a season's worth of grass grown up around it. The hay rake leaned against the equipment shed.

She did not know how long she stood there.

"Don't make that face, Lila Grace," Mae said. Lila turned back. Her grandmother watched her quietly. "Like I said. We need a conversation."

Mae took the next step up. Lila let her, kept a hand a quarter inch off her back, and followed.

The screen door creaked exactly the way it had creaked when Lila was nine and ten and twelve. The same note. The same complaint.

The dishes sat in the sink, dust on the windowsill. The wilting plant hanging in the window. A stain she'd noticed on the right hand panel of the gingham curtains on Christmas Eve was still there.

Mae went straight for her chair at the kitchen table. She lowered herself into it as if she had been considering the maneuver for a while.

"I'd like a glass of water and my lotion from the bathroom," she said.

Lila frowned. She'd brought Mae her lotion to the hospital and had put it on her hands and arms this morning. "Yes, ma'am."

"And don't fuss with food. I'm not hungry yet."

"I'm not fussing."

"You're fussing, Sugar."

Lila set Mae's overnight bag on the bench by the door and pulled the purple tube of lotion out. She handed it to Mae then made her a glass of ice water.

Mae looked up. "Quit hovering."

She pulled out the chair across from her. Mae uncapped the lotion and squeezed a dallop on her hand. Lila closed her eyes and breathed in the smell. A wave of exhaustion ran through her. She hadn't slept since...what day was it again? She was pretty sure it was still Saturday. She hadn't slept since Thursday night.

Mae reached for the lazy susan in the middle of the table and turned it. Two envelopes were tucked between the salt and pepper and the napkin holder. She plucked them up and held them out to Lila.

"Bank first," Mae said. "Then the other one."

Lila slid the page out of the envelope with the Community Federal Bank logo in the corner. The final demand before foreclosure of fifty thousand dollars made Lila's mouth go dry.

Mae had three months to get it paid. Three months. Lila looked at the number again and it stopped being a number. It was the porch and the fields and every year Mae had spent making this dirt mean something. It was the only home her grandmother had ever wanted.

"Don used the words 'reasonable accommodation,'" Mae said. "That's what they say when the answer is not yet but soon."

Lila set the letter down. She pressed it flat with one hand, as if it might curl and float away. "How did this happen?"

"I missed last year's harvest, Sugar. You know that part. The doctor in February said no heavy labor through the spring. I had no labor to hire by the time my hand healed enough to drive. The whole field went unharvested. The seed company took back the contract. I lost the deposit. I lost the buyer. I lost the year."

"That was last fall. Why am I just now hearing about this?"

Mae held Lila's eyes. "I said I'd taken a soft year."

"A soft year is not fifty thousand dollars, Mae."

"No. It is not."

Lila put both hands flat on the table on either side of the letter. Her thumbnail had a chip in it. She had a manicurist appointment Monday morning that she needed to cancel. She made herself breathe slowly.

"Why didn't you call me?"

"Because if I called you, you'd come."

"That's the answer to a different question."

"It's the answer to the only question that matters." Mae's voice did not rise. It had never risen in Lila's whole life that she could remember. "If I called you, you'd come home for a piece of dirt and a bank letter. I wanted you to come home for me."

Lila opened her mouth. Then quietly closed it again. Her eyes stung before she understood why.

"Now you've come home for me," her grandmother said. "We can do the dirt and the bank letter."

The afternoon light came in low across the table. It caught the second envelope where Mae had laid it. The second envelope was a heavier, cream-colored paper. The return address was printed in raised letters at the upper left corner that said Whitfield Development, LLC.

Inside was a single sheet folded in thirds, a developer's letterhead at the top and a developer's signature at the bottom. The body was three short paragraphs of an offer to purchase Mae's fifteen acres for a price that made her mouth drop open. She set the page down on top of the bank letter and sat back slowly in her chair.

"Two hundred forty thousand dollars," Mae said, in case Lila had not gotten there. "For the whole farm. House, fields, equipment shed, the road frontage, the pasture out back. Everything but the section the easement runs through, which they don't want. He came out himself and walked the property in May. Brought his wife once. She was nice. I enjoyed talking to her about their move from California."

"Did he know about the bank?"

"He knew enough. People in this town know what people are carrying."

Lila looked down at the cream paper. Her brain was doing the math without her permission. Two hundred forty thousand would pay off the bank and leave over one hundred and eighty. Mae could move into a small house in town and have cash to spare. She'd never turn over another sunflower in her life.

She hated the math.

"Have you agreed?" Lila said.

"No. I said I'd think about it." She laid her hand on top of Lila's. "I've thought about it for two months, Lila-girl. It's been about the only thing on my mind lately and I'm not the one who gets to decide it."

Lila's eyes burned. "Mae."

"This farm has been in my name for fifty-one years. It will be in your name longer than that, if you want it to be. It's the only thing of mine worth a thing." Mae's thumb moved on the back of Lila's hand. "It'll be yours. So you decide."

Chapter 3

Jake's hand sat heavy on the gear shift as he maneuvered the baler over the cut hay.

Jake clocked his fifth hour of work at eight-thirty on Sunday morning. He slept badly and started at three-thirty instead of four, with a lot to make up after the days he'd spent at the hospital with Mae.

Not that he minded doing anything for Mae.

The Kubota labored up the last forty yards of the rise, hay trailer dragging behind to Mae's lower acres. He'd cut them yesterday on the Kubota, now he ran the baler over them. Mae always generously gave him the hay out of the field if he did the work. She'd gotten rid of the goats she'd fed with the hay years ago. Now he kept her supplied in fresh milk whenever she wanted some in exchange for a field of hay that helped feed his dairy cows.

As he turned a corner, the upper field came alive in the morning light. The rows were as bad up close as they'd looked from the road for two months. Sparse, leaning, some plants short, some plants barely a plant at all.

His eyes ran over the rows and stopped at the gate, spotting Lila. His heart suddenly picked up steam and sweat beaded on his upper lip. He stopped the tractor and hopped out. Might as well get it over with.

She was halfway up the gate, one boot on the bottom rail, hands on the top rail, looking out at the rows. Her auburn hair blew around her face in the morning wind, catching the light, the red highlights burning bright.

The last eleven years dissipated like steam. The last time she'd seen him, he'd come to Lexington to have lunch with her at her school. His parents had been dead for six months, and he'd struggled through grief, through fear, learning how to parent his teenaged brother and how to run a farm his great-grandfather had started in 1944.

He'd been hurting, angry. He should have been with her at school, studying farming and agriculture. Not learning how to budget for groceries and cattle feed.

He realized much later that she was hurting, too; that she was homesick, scared, missing his parents in her own way.

They hadn't ended well.

He could tell when she spotted him. Her shoulders went back slightly, her chin lifted just so. For a moment, the time disappeared and they were meeting at the gate like they used to.

"Morning," she said, turning fully toward him.

He wanted to grab her by the arms and shake her and demand to know why she'd never come home. "Morning."

He looked at the sunflowers instead of at her. Easier. Fresh-cut hay hung in the air, dusty and warm. Even though he'd had a couple of days to prepare, he hadn't worked out what he'd say to her when he saw her. The words jumbled around in his head.

She turned and slung her arms back over the rail. She stood close enough that he could see the freckles on the bridge of her nose. He remembered trying to kiss each one.

"Mae told me. About the hay." She paused. "Well, about the goats and then the hay."

"Seems like something you'd have known," he said.

She raised an eyebrow. "Seems like." She pulled her arms forward, then crossed them over her chest. Instead of looking at him, she stared at the ground, watching her booted toe dig in the dirt. "Jake," she said.

That was the first time he'd heard her say his name in over a decade. "Lila."

She breathed out, and he felt it more than heard it. "Would you buy the farm?"

He took his eyes off field. "I beg your pardon?"

" From Mae. The easement section ties straight to your back pasture. You could run more cows. You could plant corn on the upper field for Waller. You wouldn't even have to put up a new barn."

She'd clearly done the math. However, he'd done that same math himself, more than once, sitting at his own kitchen table after Mae told him and Charlie about the bank letter.

"No," he said.

She looked up at him and waited. When she realized he clearly had no intention of elaborating, she stuck her chin out. "Why?"

"Well," he said, leaning his hip against the fence. "There are a couple of reasons." He paused to try to word it rationally when nothing rational was happening inside his brain right now. "First one. I don't have that kind of money sitting in a drawer. Not without mortgaging my land. And, I'm unwilling to do that."

She nodded once and continued to wait.

"Second." He sighed and looked back at the rows. "This is your grandmother's farm."

"I know whose farm it is, Jake."

He took his cap off and ran a hand through his hair then settled the cap back down "This is your inheritance. I'm not taking that from you."

She looked at the field. The day began heating up and the sunflowers didn't look like they could handle the heat wave. They needed a good summer shower. Maybe that would come tomorrow.

She was quiet a moment, like she was turning something over in her mind "Cole could do it," she murmured, half to herself. "Cole could write a check tomorrow."

He hadn't been ready to hear that name in the daylight from her own mouth. He slipped his hands into his pockets and fisted them.

"You want to sell your family's land to a jazzy country singer who was raised in Newark, New Jersey?"

"No." She shook her head and bit out the response. "I just feel desperate."

He straightened. "I'm sorry I can't help you." He gestured at the tractor. "I need to finish baling this hay. Tell Mae I'll collect the bales tomorrow if I don't get them today."

She pulled her hair back and tied it in a knot. It fascinated him that she could do that, that it stayed just like that. "I'll figure out a way so that she can stay on this land," she said.

He looked down at her, glad his hands were in his pockets, because what he wanted to do was trace her jawline and see if her skin was as soft as it used to be. "If anyone can figure it out, Lila Grace, it's you."

Tears filled her eyes and she looked toward the sad rows of flowers. "Thanks," she whispered.

He headed back to the tractor and didn't look behind him.

Lila pressed the phone harder against her ear like that would speed the network up. She leaned with her back against the counter and waited a little impatiently for the coffee to finish brewing while listening to Ella's voice in full crisis mode.

Ella took an audible breath. "Okay. So. Cassidy went on Instagram Live last night around eleven."

"And?"

"I'll text you the link to the Reel," Ella said.

"I can't open a Reel. There's no Wi-Fi here and I have almost no cell service." Lila looked at Mae's old wall phone then at the gingham curtain. The plant she'd watered yesterday had come back to life. "Just describe it."

"She did an impression of Hank Mosley."

Lila pressed her fingers against the bridge of her nose. She pictured the host of Country Now, one of the most popular podcasts about the country music industry.

Three words from him in the right tone could make or break a rising star before anyone had ever even heard her sing. "Tell me it was a soft impression. Tell me she did the cowboy hat and the deep voice and it was cute and he'll laugh it off and maybe even play it."

After a pause, Ella said, "Yeah. It was not a soft impression."

"Give me a second." She set the phone down and gripped the counter with both hands. She stared out at the struggling sunflower field and tracked the shadow of a hawk circling from above. She'd certainly had better mornings. First Jake, then...

She picked her phone back up. "Tell me."

"It was a four-minute impression and she got into the way he says her name. With the inflection. And the chuckle."

"What else?"

"She said, in his voice, that if a song made it past Hank Mosley, it had been first inspected by his fishing tackle box and approved by his second wife."

Mae came into the kitchen and slid carefully into a chair. She was moving so gingerly, as if she stepped too hard, something would crumble. Lila's mind spun between Mae and the farm and Nashville. She didn't even know where to start.

"Has Hank seen it?" she asked.

"Yes. Hank's producer called me at six this morning. Well, he called you, but we had your phone forwarded to mine. They want a discussion before the Tuesday slot."

"How many shares is it at?"

"Forty-one thousand and counting. The country subreddit picked it up overnight."

The hawk swooped and hit the ground, coming up with something in its claws. "What does Cassidy say?"

"Cassidy has not answered her phone. She must not be a morning person. I've left her two voicemails and several texts."

Lila put the phone on speaker and poured Mae a cup of coffee. She set it in front of her and then leaned back against the counter. Her mind ran through a dozen scenarios.

"All right," she said. "I'm going to draft a holding statement. Go to Hank's producer with it before they go to anybody else. I want to be in the room before the room makes a decision about us."

"You left your laptop here. Do you have access to a computer?"

That stopped her. Did she? "Good point. I need you to overnight my laptop to me. Arrange for a Starlink, too."

"Yes, ma'am."

"In the meantime, I'll dictate it to you. Let me think about it and I'll call you back."

She hung up without waiting for confirmation and opened the drawer under the phone, pulling out a yellow legal pad that had a shopping list written in Mae's script.

"Lila Grace," Mae said. "It's Sunday, Sugar."

She grabbed a ballpoint pen and took the chair across from Mae. She flipped to a clean page then looked at her grandmother. "I know it's Sunday."

"Granny Mae, I love you. This is my job."

Mae blew on the surface of her coffee but set it down without taking a drink. "The world will turn without you between now and Monday morning."

"If only." Lila stared at Mae's face and tried to remember when she'd aged. She did not seem this frail or old at Christmas. "The country music industry does not take Sundays off."

"Maybe they should. Life is short."

She stood and took her phone outside. The silence here reminded her how loud it was from her apartment balcony in the city. It came at her out of order. Mae's heart, the bank, Cassidy live on Instagram at eleven at night, no WiFi to do a thing about any of it. And Jake, who she wasn't going to think about.

Tension crawled up her neck and spread along her temple. She suddenly realized she couldn't do this. She swiped at her phone and tapped Katy's name.

Katy answered on the first ring. "I already heard."

Lila closed her eyes. "I'm handling that. But that's not why I'm calling."

A pause. Lila could picture Katy on the back deck of her house in East Nashville, coffee in one hand, dog at her feet, the news in three tabs opened on her tablet.

"I'm listening," Katy said.

"I need a couple of months."

Katy did not say anything. Lila felt safe to continue. "Mae's heart is real," she said, her voice thickening as tears flooded her throat. "She only has three months to clear a fifty-thousand-dollar debt or the bank's taking the farm. She's seventy-six years old…" Lila's words broke, raw and trembling. "I can't…"

She swallowed hard, fighting to keep her voice steady. "I need to do what I can to help her, and I can't do that and work my job."

"What about Cassidy's launch?" Katy asked.

It was a fair question. "Ella will be my proxy. I can run Cassidy's launch from here. I drafted the entire campaign already. It's actually executable without me in the room."

"And anything that breaks like Cassidy broke last night?"

"We have systems in place. It's all very organized. There's very little someone can do that I haven't created a template on how to handle it." She sniffled and wiped her eyes. "I can do some things. I just can't do it all."

The line was quiet for a moment. She could almost see the thoughts crossing Katy's face. Finally, she said, "Two months. Not a full sabbatical, but part-time. If a fire starts, you put it out from there. We cannot lose the relationships you built. Do you understand what I mean?"

"I understand."

"Take care of your grandmother, Lila. That should be your priority for the next two months. We'll be here when you come back."

The line went quiet. Lila sank onto a rocking chair and set her phone on the ground in front of her. She pressed her heels against her eyes but that did nothing to stop the flow of tears. Relief mixed with worry. A part of her wanted to stay folded in that chair until none of it was true anymore.

When she felt like she had control of the swirl of emotion, she wiped her face with her fingertips, then picked her phone back up and went back inside. Mae was where she left her. The coffee looked untouched.

"My boss has agreed to let me work part time from here for two months," she said.

Mae stared at her with watery eyes then nodded and pointed at the legal pad. "Best get that thing handled."

She slowly stood. "I'm going to go read in my chair." She walked with careful steps into the front room. Lila picked up her pen again and after a moment of listening to Mae settle into her recliner, she started drafting a plan.

Chapter 4

Lila slid the napkin dispenser into the corner of the booth and propped her phone against it.

The dispenser caught on the rim of her iced-tea glass. She wiped the ring of water the iced tea had sweated onto the formica. The air conditioning in the Hollow Diner worked well and the WiFi had a strong signal. Two things she couldn't say about Mae's kitchen on a hundred-degree Sunday in July.

Her thumb was already in motion.

Ella's text had landed five minutes ago:

Cassidy awake. mortified. wants to call you.

Lila typed back.

Let her sit with it. I'll talk to her tomorrow.

She set the phone face-down on the formica and reached for the tea. She pictured Hank Mosley's face. Three words from him in the right tone could end Cassidy before she'd sung her first verse on the air. At this point, sixty-nine thousand shares meant Cassidy had already given Hank three words in the wrong tone. His producer had asked for a discussion. The discussion would be a price. Lila had paid prices like that before. Except this time, she couldn't do it in person and make sure the remorse got portrayed correctly.

The phone buzzed against the formica.

> Hank's producer will take a call Wednesday.

Lila exhaled slowly.

> Good. set it after the Tuesday slot. I want him to hear Cassidy live before he hears her contrite.

She thumbed send. Pressed the heels of her hands into her eyes.

The bell over the door rang. She lowered her hands and spotted Mae's friend Louise Tate. Mrs. Tate saw Lila before Lila could pretend not to see her. She came across the diner with both hands held out.

"Lila Grace." She took Lila's hand in both of hers like she was checking for a temperature. "When did you get back, honey? How's Mae?"

"Thursday night," Lila said. "She came home from the hospital yesterday afternoon."

Mrs. Tate let go of Lila's hand. She tucked both of her own under her chin. "And you?"

She smiled. "Well, Mae had me worried for a bit, but I'm well now. It's nice to be here for a while." Which was all true, even if she felt split between two worlds.

Mrs. Tate held that for a beat. "I'll be by with a chicken pot pie tomorrow morning."

"She'll be glad to see you," Lila said. "I'm sure she'll enjoy talking to someone other than me."

"I'll be glad to see her." Mrs. Tate patted Lila's hand once more. She moved on toward the counter. Her pie was already in a clamshell waiting on her.

Lila watched her go. And remembered the last time she'd seen her. Christmas Eve at the post office. They'd had a brief conversation, mostly about Mae. Being a Harper in Fox Hollow still meant the same thing it had eleven years ago: everyone knew her name before she gave it. She loved that so many familiar places filled the spaces in this town. In Nashville, she was so anonymous in most places.

The phone buzzed.

> Statement up. Cassidy linked it from her stories. Shares slowing.

She slid out of the booth. The waitress caught her eye from the pass-through and Lila held up her empty glass; the waitress nodded.

The hallway to the restroom ran along the back of the diner past the counter. Lila walked it slowly. Her hip had locked up after an hour in the booth. She passed the bulletin board next to the swinging kitchen door.

Then she stopped. Walked back two steps.

The bulletin board covered six feet of wall space, filled with business cards pegged by thumbtacks, and flyers announcing a 5K for the volunteer fire department, a lost cat named Biscuit, a hay-cutting service over toward Versailles. And in the middle, in two colors of marker on yellow posterboard:

FOX HOLLOW FALL KICKOFF FESTIVAL. LABOR DAY WEEKEND. SATURDAY BOOTHS THROUGH MONDAY PARADE. LIVE BLUEGRASS

SATURDAY EVENING ON THE COURTHOUSE GAZEBO. VOLUNTEERS WELCOME — SIGN SHEET AT THE DINER COUNTER.

Lila read it twice.

The festival was an all-day event on the Saturday of Labor Day weekend. She spent all of her life working with Mae in her booth selling sunflowers and various sunflower related paraphernalia. The Friday before that, hotels would be filled with guests and vendors. The Bourbon Trail would pull even more people in.

Her mind began strategizing, planning, deciding.

Mae's sunflower banner heads always made it through Labor Day. The rows would be sparse, but the flowers would be in full bloom. A field, a backdrop, a place for cameras.

She thought of a stage in front of a sunflower field. Food vendors, merchandise vendors. A band that would draw a crowd.

She thought of the bands she knew personally. She thought, against her own will, of one specific band.

Don't.

She thought of him anyway. Cole had called her his muse three times the night she broke up with him. He'd also said, "Lila, if you ever need anything, please call me. I love you." That had been four months ago.

Would he still mean it?

Of course he would. Bad behavior aside, she knew he did love her.

She walked back to the booth without going to the restroom.

The waitress had refilled the iced tea. Lila flipped to a blank page in the yellow notepad she'd taken from Mae's house.

Friday night. Sunflower field. Whisky Rebellion.
Stage rental, Louisville. Sound and lights.
Permits at the courthouse Monday. Insurance.
Online ticketing. Sponsors (ask Waller).
Concessions. Merch.

She wrote without lifting the pen.

She started a second column for the math, then stopped. She knew the math in Nashville, not central Kentucky. But it was going to work. She'd been doing this math, in different denominations, for seven years. It would work.

She finally set the pen down. She'd filled two pages on the notepad. After making a couple of additional notes on top of the ones already there, she reached for her phone.

"Anything else, hon?" The waitress was at her elbow with the iced-tea pitcher.

"The check, please," Lila said. "And whatever this slice of coconut cream pie is over by the window, can I get one to go for my grandmother?"

"Honey, I'll send her two slices. On the house. You tell her Charlene says get well and we love her."

Lila had to swallow before she could answer. "I will," she said.

The waitress turned for the register. Lila scrolled down her contacts. Past Carter, Ella. Past Charlie. To Cole.

She paid in cash and tipped well. She took the bag from the waitress and stepped out into the July heat. she paused and looked up at the clouds forming in the sky. The clouds were building toward rain, maybe a break in this heat at last. Mae had the AC unit installed when Lila came to live with her. It could not keep up with the heat.

Across the square the courthouse copper dome was greening at the seams. A pickup went past with hay sticking out of the bed. She looked down at her phone and pressed the call button.

Jake hefted a fifty-pound bag of dairy ration onto his shoulder and walked it from the storage room to the bed of his truck.

He set it down and went back in for another. He had eight bags to load and Charlie was working the dolly behind him, carrying two bags at a time, so they'd be done in twelve minutes if neither of them said anything stupid.

The Sunday afternoon sun came in slanted through the open bay door of the Feed and Seed. The concrete was hot. Jake's shirt stuck to his back. Mae's lower acres would want a third hauling tomorrow morning if the heat held. The hay would be brittle by the loft.

He turned to walked back in for another bag when he heard Lila's voice.

She was on the phone, on the other side of the parking lot with her back to him. Her hair was up in the same messy knot she'd worn at the gate this morning.

"Cole. Hey." A pause. "Yeah. I'm in Kentucky."

Jake set the bag down in the truck bed maybe a little harder than the bag deserved. Irritation prickled up his neck as he went back for another.

"It's a long story. Mae had a heart attack." Another pause. She was smiling into the phone. "She's fine. She's home. Yes. I know. No. No, listen..."

Her voice faded as he went inside. When he returned, she was still on the phone.

"Friday night would be amazing. Yeah. I know!" She paused then laughed at something Cole said.

Jake walked back for another bag. He stood in the doorway and counted to ten before going back out there.

"I just need you to say yes and I'll cover the rest of it."

Charlie came out of the side bay with the dolly. He took one look at Jake's face and stopped.

"What?"

"Nothing."

Charlie set the dolly down and looked over Jake's shoulder. "I see."

He looked back at Jake and didn't say anything.

Jake helped Charlie unload the two bags.

"Cole. Cole, you're being ridiculous. Stop." She was laughing softer now. "I know. I know you do. And, thank you. I mean it." Pause. "Yeah. I'll call you tomorrow."

She slipped the phone into her pocket and turned. When she saw them, she waved and walked over.

"Hey, Lila," Charlie said. "Welcome home."

Her face broke open. It was the brightest thing Jake had seen all weekend. "Charlie. Look at you."

"Look at me, what."

"Look at you running the whole place."

"Most days I just unlock the door." Charlie pulled her into a one-arm hug like a brother. Lila laughed and put a hand on his shoulder. "How's Mae?"

"Home." If Jake hadn't been watching her face so closely, he might have missed the shadow that crossed it.

"You know, Jake and I usually have an early supper with her on Sundays." He raised an eyebrow. "So..."

Lila slapped his chest and stepped away from him. "I am not making you two dinner. If you want to bring something over, you're welcome."

Charlie chuckled. "I'm just kidding. I mean, we do normally go there, but we didn't plan to today."

Jake leaned against the truck. "She doing okay? She looked so frail in the hospital. I'm trying to remember if that started before."

She shook her head. "She didn't look like this at Christmas. I wondered if the heart attack did it to her or if she was sick leading up to it." She tucked a strand of wayward hair behind her ear. "There's signs that she'd started to let things like simple housework go. I wish I'd been here for her."

He opened his mouth to condemn her absence but Charlie cut him off. "She's the first to say that you're doing what you love. There is no room for anything other than being thankful you can be here now."

"Yeah."

Jake walked back for another sack. Their voices kept up behind him. Charlie asked about Nashville. Lila answered. Charlie laughed at whatever she said. Jake picked up the next bag, walked it to the truck, set it in the bed. Went back for the next.

When he came out with the seventh, Charlie had stepped inside for a clipboard. She was still there. Her eyes were on Jake. He put the bag in the back of the truck and turned. She was still staring at him.

"Something on my shirt or something?"

Her eyes looked down at his chest then back up at him. "Are you alright?"

"Hot day for hauling feed."

She wasn't moving on. "Is that it?"

He raised an eyebrow. "Did you have anything else in mind?"

When she opened and closed her mouth, he went back in for the final bag of feed. When he came back out, Charlie had returned. He held out the clipboard to him, and Jake signed the bill for the feed.

"You need anything, Lila, or did you just come over to say hi?" Charlie asked.

"Cat food. Mae said you'd know what to give me."

"Sure thing. Give me a sec." Charlie disappeared inside again.

Jake slammed the tailgate shut and rounded on her. He could afford to look at her now. He'd caught one side of a phone call across thirty feet of pavement — a name, a laugh, a Friday night — and his chest had already filled in the rest. Maybe he had it wrong. He didn't feel like he had it wrong. He told himself he was almost grateful to quit wondering, and didn't believe that either.

"Charlie and I take care of Mae. She's the family we have left."

A muscle ticked in her jaw. "I'm sure she appreciates that. I know I do."

"Well, I don't want to step on any of your toes. So, you let me know if you want us to hang back while you're home or if you want us to keep doing what we do."

Charlie returned with a bag of cat food and the clipboard. He held the board out to her first and showed her where to sign the food to Mae's account. "Does Mae have a balance, Charlie?"

A pained look tightened his lips. "I think you should check with Mae."

"Oh." She said the word on a breath. "I'm sorry. I'm trying to get an idea of all of the numbers."

"Well, when she gives her approval, you and I can have a sit down."

Jake almost smiled. Charlie was two years younger than them, was only fifteen the last time she'd seen him. Jake reckoned that she still thought of him that way. In truth, his store was well-run. A tight ship that he took very seriously.

"Oh, uh, thanks." She traded the clipboard for the bag. "I'm sorry if I offended."

"Not at all. And I'm sure Mae won't mind. But that's up to her." He threw an arm over her shoulders and hugged her against his side. "So good to see you."

"You as well." She turned and started walking to her car but after about three steps, she turned and looked at Jake. "See y'all around."

Chapter 5

The latch on the holding gate stuck, and Jake worked it with the heel of his hand until the iron gave. He'd just finished hosing down the milking parlor. The bulk tank's compressor softly ticked. The tanker from the dairy was due at ten tomorrow morning. He pulled his cap off, ran his sleeve across his forehead, and set the cap back on. The wind shifted out of the west and brought him the bourbon sweetness of the Waller fields two miles off.

He had a couple of hours of daylight left, but not a lot of energy. He decided he'd relax this evening instead of finding a chore to do. There would always be more chores to do. He crossed the yard and went into his kitchen. He'd tossed chicken and rice into the crockpot earlier. It smelled good, but he wasn't quite hungry yet, so he grabbed a cold beer out of the refrigerator and went out onto the porch just as Lila started up the steps.

He raised an eyebrow. "To what do I owe this pleasure?"

She smirked. "Got another one of those?"

He held the beer out to her then went back inside and got himself one. Soon, they sat across from each other in his mother's wicker rockers. "You walk all the way over here for the view?"

She took a small sip of beer then rolled the bottle between her hands. "Granny Mae sent me. She said if I didn't tell you tonight, she'd walk out here in her bedroom slippers and tell you herself."

"I'd believe her, too."

"That's why I came." She leaned back in her chair. "You done for the day or am I keeping you?"

He set his beer against his denim clad thigh and rocked backward. "What did Granny Mae send you to tell me?"

A breath of wind lifted the loose hair at her temple. She tucked it back. He had been watching her tuck her hair like that since she was eleven. He had never learned to look away.

"I have an idea," she said. "To save Mae's place."

"You've always been good with ideas."

Her eyes widened, as if the compliment surprised her. She cleared her throat and set the bottle on the porch railing. "I want to have a concert the Friday night before the autumn festival. We get a couple of sponsors, get a mid-tier group so that we don't overwhelm with too many people but one popular enough that I know we'd sell out. We'd clear enough to handle the bank note. If we made it a regular thing, there's so much we could do with it."

He looked out at the fence that ran along Mae's field. "Where?"

"The lower acres where you have the hay field."

He set the beer down and walked to the end of the porch, leaning his shoulder against the railing and looked out over the fields. The lowing of a cow sounded in the evening air. "What group?"

"Whisky Rebellion." She paused and his neck muscles tightened. "Cole Banks. I managed his brand work on two tours through Starboard. I called in a favor this afternoon. His manager is supposed to call me tomorrow."

"I see." He took a sip of beer to wet his suddenly dry mouth. Cole Banks. The name had a specific weight he didn't feel like examining.

"It came together fast. Once I had a plan." She stood and walked up to him, resting her hip on the railing.

He looked down at her. "What did Mae say?"

"'This farm has hosted weddings and funerals, Lila-girl. It can host a concert.'"

He smiled despite himself. Then he looked out again and thought of a couple thousand people filling that space and the smile faded. He thought of a thousand people in that hay field and felt everything in him resist. Then he thought of Mae. If he could do anything to help Mae, he would. He'd said that. He meant it.

"Twenty-ninth." He worked the date through, the weeks between, the parade of things that would have to happen in those weeks. "That's not much time."

"I know it isn't." She slipped her hands into her jeans pockets. "Sponsors I can pull from the Starboard list. Waller will sponsor. I'm almost sure of that already. He contacted me about doing something like this a few years ago. I just never focused on it to come back to him. I checked today and he isn't already involved with a music festival or anything, so I feel good about it." She put a hand to her chest. "I'm sorry. I'm babbling. I've been thinking and plotting all day and there are a million details happening in my mind right now."

"How many people?" he asked.

"A thousand. Twelve hundred at the very outside."

He did not answer her right away. He took his cap off, ran a hand back through his hair, set the cap on. He did not let himself look at the careful hopeful set of her mouth, or at the familiar way she had said the name Cole.

"It's a smart plan, Lila Grace."

Her shoulders eased. The smile that lit her face could have left a shadow. "It really is." She pushed away from the rail. "Listen. We'll keep the crowd off the parlor side. We'll fence it. Hire security. You won't even know they're—"

"I trust you."

That stopped her mid-sentence. She put a hand on his arm. "Thank you, Jake."

He nodded. "I don't trust twelve hundred people coming. But I trust you and I know you'll work out the details." He drained his beer. "Best get back before the sun goes down. You don't know the path like you used to."

⟵⸻◦◦⸻⟶

The bell on the tasting-room door of the Waller Distillery rang the way she remembered it ringing in high school, the day her senior class had toured the floor for science credit and she had stood in the back beside Jake while Travis Waller explained the grain bill like he had been born to it. Because he had. The sign over the door still said WALLER BOURBON, EST. 1898, four generations down, fifth working the floor.

Two heads turned.

"Look what the wind blew in." Travis sat at the long bar, a pair of Glencairn glasses in front of him and a clipboard in his hand. He was thicker through the chest than she remembered, sun-marked around the eyes, his hair the same wheat color and his smile exactly what it had always been. "Lila Harper. Get over here."

She crossed the floor and let him pull her into a hug that smelled like warm oak and a clean shirt. Behind him, Jake set his cap straight on his head and did not get up from the bar stool.

"Travis." She squeezed his shoulder and stepped back to look at him. "How's your mama liking Florida?"

"She's here now. She can't stand the summer there." Travis pulled at the cuff of a sleeve already rolled to the elbow. "She does her best to keep me in line."

"Then explain the beard."

"It's a good beard. Don't lie to me."

Lila laughed. The sound came out lighter than she expected. She glanced at Jake, who barely tipped his cap an inch.

"Bradford." She said it the way she had said it a thousand times. "Bit early for a tasting."

"I'm on hour six of my day." He picked up the Glencairn glass and swirled the amber liquid.

She glanced at the clock above the bar. "At ten in the morning?"

"Cows wait for no man, Lila Grace."

Travis put the clipboard down. "Pull up a stool, Lila. Coffee?"

"Please. Black."

She set the iPad and the folder on the bar, took the stool one over from Jake, and rested her elbows on the warm cedar of the bar top. The smell of the place was still the smell she remembered, sweet grain and oak char and the faint metal note of the still warming up across the wall.

"All right," Travis said, sliding a mug in front of her. "I am sitting down. I have my coffee. Tell me what brings you to my floor at nine in the morning on a Monday. And please say a concert or music festival that I can slap my beautiful branding onto."

"A concert."

He didn't blink. "Tell me more."

"Friday before the Fall Kickoff festival. I've confirmed Whisky Rebellion to play a full outdoor concert in Mae's lower acres. I'm thinking twelve hundred seats, ticketed."

"Whisky Rebellion." Travis's eyes briefly cut sideways to Jake.

"Waller as the title sponsor?" he asked. "Like, Waller Bourbon Presents: Whisky Rebellion."

"That's what I'm thinking."

Travis looked at her for a long beat, then set the clipboard aside. "You know I've been wanting to do this. But I want to know if Mae wasn't about to lose her farm, would you be coming to me with this?"

That was a good question. She owed her friend an honest answer. "Probably not today. But on my desk in my office is a bright pink notecard reminding me to remember Waller Bourbon whenever an opportunity like this comes. I've not ignored you. It's just never been something that has crossed my desk yet."

He leaned both forearms on the bar. "My grandfather raised that corn on Bradford ground for thirty years before Jake's daddy was old enough to drive the tractor. My family has poured Bradford corn into Waller mash bills since before either of us was born. You walking in here with this is not a sponsorship, Lila."

She did not trust her voice for a second. She lifted the coffee. "So that's a yes."

"That's a yes wearing its Sunday clothes." He laughed and slapped the bar. "We're in. Whatever you need. Title slot, banner placement, a tasting tent on the field, our truck for the staging haul if you don't have one already, my email list goes out tomorrow morning. We'll cut you a number by close of business that lets you book the stage rental without flinching."

She did not look at Jake. She did not have to. He was there, not speaking, the way he had been at fence lines and bonfires and in the bleachers of the gym when she was sixteen.

"Travis."

"Don't." He was still laughing. "Don't do the marketing thank-you. Just say yes, this is happening, and let's go work."

"Yes. This is happening." She grinned and slapped his upraised hand in a high-five.

From across the bar, Jake set his mug down. "I should go," he said. "Cows."

"Bradford." Travis looked at him. "We're not done."

"You and I aren't." Jake stood and pulled his keys out of his pocket. "I'll come back when she's gone."

"Fair." Travis turned back to Lila.

Jake nodded once at her and walked out. The bell on the door rang.

Travis looked at her with both eyebrows up and his mouth set very, very neutral.

"What?" she asked, feeling heat crawling up her neck.

He shrugged with both palms up. "I am a sponsor. I am a professional. Sponsors do not weigh in on personal arrangements." He held the line for another beat. "Travis Waller does, however."

"I wish I could fix whatever is wrong with Jake and how he feels toward me, but I can't."

"Well," he said, drawing out the word in two syllables. "You crushed his heart. It's never really been recovered."

Her eyes stung. "Well, a lot of things were out of my control then. His folks were gone. I was drowning. A lot of words got said that shouldn't have. He wasn't the only one with a broken heart."

Travis cleared his throat then pulled a yellow legal pad out from under the bar and clicked his pen.

"Walk me through your draw," he said. "Where do you want me on the marquee."

She talked. Travis took notes in his careful angled handwriting. The light moved across the limestone wall. By the time she stood and gathered her iPad and her folder, her phone showed three missed calls. One from Cole's manager. One from Ella. One from a 502 number she did not know.

She walked back out into the parking lot and slipped into her car. She turned the car on to get the air conditioning flowing then pressed return on the 502 number. It rang twice.

"Lila Harper, this is Bryce Linville with Cole Banks's management. We were hoping to walk you through the proposed concert on August twenty-ninth. Do you have ten minutes?"

She had as many minutes as he needed. "I have ten minutes."

Chapter 6

Lila climbed the courthouse steps with the folder pinned under her arm. The limestone gave back the morning heat. Above her the copper dome caught the sun and threw it down.

She pushed through the brass-handled door into the cool of the lobby. Permits Office, the door said. End of the hall, second on the right.

The clerk at the desk had pearl earrings and pin-curled gray hair. Her nameplate introduced her as Opal Henry. "Lila Harper," she said before Lila opened her mouth. "Mae's girl. Sit down, honey."

"Yes, ma'am." Lila slid the folder onto the counter and turned it so the woman could read the top page.

"I need to know what permits I need for an outdoor concert at Granny Mae's farm."

Opal made a pencil note down the side of the form. "We need the assembly use form, the temporary noise variance, and the food-vendor stamp if you've got concession booths."

"I will."

"All right." She slid three forms across the counter and picked up the desk phone. "Mayor likes to know."

While Lila waited for the mayor, she thumbed through the forms and made sure she didn't have any special questions. A few minutes later, a door opened behind Opal and Mayor Caldwell came out. He took the folder and scanned the top page carefully. "Twelve hundred people. On a sunflower field."

"Yes, sir."

He turned a page. "You've got six weeks."

"Five and change."

His pencil came off his ear and he wrote a small note in the margin. "That's a lot of work in five and change."

"It is." She didn't apologize for it.

He turned to the second page. "Title sponsor?"

"Waller Bourbon." She smiled. "Travis has been wanting to do a concert for a while."

"I know. We've talked about it." A small dry note of approval. He signed the assembly use form quickly and slid it back. "Looking forward to it."

"Glad to hear it, Mr. Mayor."

"Wish your grandmother well from me."

He went back into his office.

Opal stamped the noise variance and slid it across. Then she pulled a sticky note off her desk and wrote a number on it. "Sound's only half. You'll need ticketing, rain insurance, equipment."

Lila nodded. "Here's my list." She opened a file folder and pulled out a stapled packet.

Opal looked through it and nodded. "Very good. Looks like you've covered all your bases." She handed the note over. "Call me if anything tangles. I've worked the festival booth desk thirty-one years."

"Thank you, ma'am."

She headed for the diner. Secured in a corner booth, a tuna salad and iced tea ordered, she worked on her shopping list. She'd receive the Starlink and her computer today. She needed a desk and a good desk chair. She added a magnetic white board and some colorful markers. That would get her started. And, it would all arrive tomorrow.

That done, she called the insurance carrier. The agent on the line was a woman in Lexington who said three sentences then went quiet to type. Lila gave her the assembly count, the venue, the title sponsor, the ticketing model, and the heat-wave forecast. The agent quoted the rider in two pieces. Lila said yes to both and asked her to email the bind.

Sound was already booked through Cole's manager. A thirty-by-twenty stage, full backline, two engineers. She checked her email and confirmed the load-in and the truck route.

Ticketing took the longest. The platform's intake guy had a Nashville accent and the patient cadence of someone who'd onboarded a hundred small-market events that summer. He walked her through the credit-card fee, the ADA seating block, the will-call printer, and the hold percentage for press. Twelve hundred capacity, twelve hundred ticket allotment. She approved each one. He asked when she wanted the on-sale to begin.

"Saturday morning."

He clicked on his keyboard then paused. "This Saturday?"

"Yes."

He laughed once. "All right, Ms. Harper. We'll be ready."

She used her tablet to answer Bryce Linville's email containing several questions and demands so that he could finalize the contract. The tuna salad appeared at her elbow as she typed and she barely glanced at it.

"How much do you need?"

Jake didn't look up from the measuring stick. The bottomland sloped down to the cottonwoods and broadened east toward the creek. He paced the rows. There was room enough for a small subdivision.

"Two hundred spaces."

"Two hundred." He set the stick on his shoulder and looked across the field. "Where's everyone else going to park?"

"There's a derelict strip mall on the bypass. Mayor Caldwell arranged with the owners of the property to provide parking spaces. I have a shuttle company that will shuttle people to and from."

She stood beside him at the edge of the row. In deference to the heat, she wore a sleeveless dress and work boots. A line of sweat slid down her back. The air felt heavy and she looked up at the sky, seeing the dark clouds forming to the west. Thank goodness.

"What are you thinking for entrance?"

"Off the river road, here. Out off the back drive, there." She pointed toward the gate. "Two flaggers, one in, one out."

She needed his help with this. She had a head for columns and figures. He had a head for spaces and structures.

"Bottomland is wet north of the cottonwood. It's only going to get wetter in August."

"I know."

He looked at her sideways. "You'll ruin it if you put cars there. Assuming they could even get out."

She grinned at him. "Like that time I got Mae's Toyota down there and you had to haul it out with your daddy's tractor before either of us got caught?"

He smirked. Her stomach did something funny. She wondered, briefly, what life would have looked like if she'd just come home from college. He set the stick down. "All right."

She stood quiet a minute. She'd asked him for a lot in three days. The lower acres for the stage. Hours of his time he didn't have.

"Jake." She stopped a step short of him and put her hand on his arm. "Thank you."

He nodded once, his eyes still on the field. He didn't say you're welcome. He said, "I'll run flags Thursday night. You won't have to worry about it."

She blinked back tears as she turned away from him. She'd come down off his porch Sunday night knowing he didn't trust twelve hundred people coming. She'd come up the bottomland tonight knowing he'd given her the parking anyway.

She walked back along the edge of the field. At the cottonwood she turned and looked at him over her shoulder. She wanted to go back to him, reset to the way they felt about each other the day before his parents crashed their little plane. She had wanted that. She'd wanted him.

Shaking her head, she kept walking. She had a good life. So did he. And they managed it apart.

✦ ∞ ✦

The compressor on the bulk tank kicked on, and Jake hosed the last of the manure off the parlor floor. The cows stood at the far end of the pasture, knee-deep in the late grass, their tails switching at the swarms of summer flies. The sky to the west had gone the color of old iron and the wind had picked up and cooled. He shut off the spigot and flipped the breaker on the lights.

Charlie's truck pulled up the gravel before he'd hung the hose.

"Hey." Charlie cut the engine and got out. "Got a minute?"

"Always." Jake stepped out of the parlor and wiped his hands on the front of his jeans.

"Lila Grace called the store looking to borrow some tools."

"Yeah?" He glanced toward Mae's place. "For what?"

"Said she's putting a desk and a chair together she got in the mail today. She needed a Phillips head and a hammer."

She'd probably figured he was still in the milking parlor. "When did she call?"

Charlie squinted at the western sky. "Half an hour ago. I told her I'd run them out after I closed."

"I'll go."

"Figured." Charlie headed toward the house. "Dinner on?"

"Leftovers in the fridge."

Jake followed Charlie to the house and went to the bathroom adjoining his bedroom. He washed up from his day, then pulled a clean shirt over his head. Back outside, he took the canvas tool roll out of the back seat of his truck and headed to Mae's house.

The path between the farms had been worn slick from his boot for twenty-some years. The first fat drops of rain hit his shoulders before he was halfway across the field.

Mae was at the kitchen table with a magazine open in front of her and a mug of coffee at her elbow. "Sugar."

"Granny Mae."

"She's in the back bedroom, son. Door's open. Pot pie's on the stove if you want a plate."

He passed through the kitchen and down the narrow hallway. The wallpaper had a faint green pattern of vines that had been there longer than him. The third door on the left stood open. He stopped in the doorframe.

The room smelled like lemon cleaner. Lila sat cross-legged on the floor with the assembly instructions spread across her lap and a screw between her teeth. She had her hair pushed up off her neck with a pencil. The desk pieces were laid out in a circle around her, the chair-in-a-box still sealed against the wall, and a magnetic whiteboard leaned next to the closet, still wrapped in plastic.

"Bradford."

"Lila Grace."

She took the screw out of her teeth. "Did Charlie tell you what I need?"

He held up the kit. "He did."

"You didn't need to drive over here."

"I walked over." He set the tool roll down on the floor and crouched. "If you'd have called me, I would have been over half an hour ago."

She narrowed her eyes. "Were you not in the midst of milking half an hour ago?"

He grinned and winked. "Where's your top piece?"

"That one." She pointed with the screwdriver. "Pre-drilled holes are on the underside. The directions say to use the dowels first, then the screws."

"I think it's safe to say that the directions are wrong."

She laughed. The sound filled the room. "Of course they are."

He held out his hand for the instructions. She handed them across, and her fingers brushed his knuckles. The rain suddenly picked up on the roof above them. He read down the page carefully once, set it aside, and reached for the long side panel.

They worked. She held the corners while he drove the screws. He set the bracket; she handed him the next piece; he flipped the whole frame upright. She knelt with both hands on the edge while he tightened the cross-rail underneath. Her hair came loose from the pencil and fell forward across her cheek and she pushed it back with her wrist because her fingers were holding a dowel. He caught the smell of her shampoo and the lemon cleaner and the rain.

"The room looks great," he said.

She looked over at the day bed. "I'm thinking about putting in a sofa bed and removing that."

He watched her look around the room then back at him. "Sounds like you're staying a while."

She raised one shoulder. "At least until September."

The lights flickered with the next round of lightning, but they stayed on. Thunder clapped. He put the last screw in and stood and held a hand down to her. She set her palm in his and let him pull her up. The desk stood on four legs in the middle of the floor. It was white with clean lines and absolutely no personality.

"Where do you want it?"

She gestured at the empty wall across from the bed. "Here. And the white board here," she said, stepping to the side and brushing the wall.

He set the screwdriver down on the lid of the empty box. "It needs anchors. Tape on the back of a board this size won't hold a week."

She crossed her arms and raised an eyebrow. "Do we have anchors?"

He toed his tool roll. "Yep." He pulled the whiteboard out of the plastic and held it up against the wall while she stepped back to look. He moved it left an inch, then up half an inch.

"There."

He set the board against the closet, took a pencil from his roll, and marked the four corners on the wall with a small X each. Then he knocked twice along the line. Hollow. He pulled a packet of drywall anchors out of the bottom of the roll, drove a pilot with the awl, set the anchor with the heel of his hand, and did the same on the other three corners. He lifted the board and held it level. She held the right side steady while he drove the screws on the left. They crossed and switched; she held the left, he drove the right.

She let go.

The board held.

He stepped back. He ran a thumb along the bottom edge to make sure it sat true. He checked placement with his level across the top then along the sides. Square. Level. Tight to the wall. He nodded once.

"I'll go ahead and get your chair built then you'll be done."

"It can wait."

He already had his knife out and had run the blade along the tape. "No reason to wait." He liked having an excuse to stay here. He showed her how to attach the arms while he put the seat on the base. In five minutes, they had the chair complete.

"Easy peasy," she said, brushing her hands.

He packed his tools back up.

"Do you want some supper?"

He shook his head. As much as he wanted to be here with her, he needed to get away. "No thank you."

The lightning flashed. She looked out the window then said, "Come out on the porch. The storm is something."

He followed her back through the kitchen. Mae was gone, to the front room, to her recliner. The screen door slapped behind them and the porch caught them both in the cool of the rain coming sideways in under the eaves.

The lightning ran along the ridge to the west and lit the sunflower rows for a half-second at a time. The thunder came on long delays. The rain sheeted down the porch posts and ran off the gutter in a single bright rope.

He stood at the top of the steps and put his hands in his pockets. She crossed to the railing and braced her palms on the wet wood and didn't say anything. The lightning lit her hair and her shoulders and the curve of her cheek, and went out, and came back, and went out. He counted the beats between the flash and the answering thunder. Five seconds. Then four. Then three.

The storm was coming closer.

She turned to him.

"Thank you, Jake."

"You don't need to thank me."

"I do." She stepped close and put her arms around him.

Before he could talk himself out of it, he pulled her in.

She fit against his chest the way she had at eighteen. Her head came up to the place under his jaw it had always come up to. Her arms went around his ribs exactly the way they'd always gone around his ribs. He silently counted three rounds of thunder while he held her, and he didn't loosen his grip on the third one.

He could have stood there until the storm passed. He didn't move his hand from the small of her back. He didn't take a breath that wasn't filled with the smell of her hair. The lightning came inside his eyelids when he closed them.

He thought about her, and what it had cost him.

I trust you, he thought. *I've always trusted you.*

She loosened first. She didn't step all the way back. She kept one hand on his chest and looked up at him with the rain behind her and her eyes wet.

The lightning lit her face white. Her eyes were the green-gold of sunflower stems at the end of August. Her eyes searched his face, then drifted across his mouth. He braced himself, afraid that she would kiss him.

Thunder rolled above the field, long and low.

Chapter 7

Jake initialed the bottom of page three and slid the contract back across the cedar bar. Travis read aloud from his own copy on the other side of the wood.

"Page four, sign and print at the foot."

Jake signed and printed.

"Page five is the per-bushel and the moisture spec. Same as last year on the per-bushel. We bumped the moisture floor a quarter-point on your insistence."

"It needs the quarter-point."

"I know it, and that's why we wrote it." Travis smiled and slid a fresh page across the wood.

The cedar bar took the early-afternoon light and held it. The copper still showed through the window over Travis's shoulder, cool now between runs. The smell of the angel share coming out of the rickhouse filled the air, warm and grain-thick.

Lila came through the gift shop into the bar. She wore a loose dress the soft yellow color of new corn. "They said you'd be in here," she said, putting sunglasses into her bag. She crossed the ornate rug, heels quiet on the intricate pattern.

"Lila Grace Harper."

"Travis." She came up to the bar easy and smiling, and Travis was around the corner of the wood and pulling her into a hug before she made the third stool. "Good to see you again."

She slid onto the stool beside him, close enough that he caught the faint trace of her perfume, something light and green, like fresh stalks after rain. The ache was still there.

She set her folder on the cedar beside Jake's contract and slid two pages out of it. "Sponsor agreement. The lawyer in Lexington emailed it back countersigned this morning."

"Perfect." Travis read the pages carefully, line by line, signed both copies, dated them, and slid one back to her. "Welcome to the Waller Bourbon Sunflower Concert."

"Thank you, Travis." She tucked her copy into the folder, and her eyes came around to Jake for the first time since the bell. "Bradford."

"Lila Grace."

He had not crossed the path to her place since the storm five days ago. She looked like she belonged here in the cool hush of dark wood and warm leather.

"Don't let me stop you," she said.

"Two more pages." He turned page seven and signed, then page eight, and signed and printed and dated.

Travis countersigned both copies, paperclipped them, and slid Jake's stack to his elbow. "Done. I'm sending the original to the lawyer Monday."

"Pleasure doing business with you."

"I have something for you," Travis said. He went around the bar and out a side door.

Jake turned and faced Lila directly. "Get your office all set up?"

"I did. And I have internet and a printer. It's like the twenty-first century came to Harper Sunflower Farm."

"Imagine that." He leaned back in the stool. "I have contemplated doing the request to get fiber optics out there, but I've never encountered a use for it and Mae didn't want any part of it."

"Well, yeah, I mean she doesn't even have a cell phone." She chuckled and tucked her hair behind her ear.

Travis returned with a quart Mason jar in his hand. The bourbon inside was a dark amber color.

"This is what I really dragged the both of you here for." He set the jar on the cedar between them. "My twelve-year-old. We're bottling this in two weeks. The labels were approved this morning. I've had the bottling line on hold twice already. Sit down with me, Bradford, and you too, Lila Grace."

Travis pulled three Glencairn glasses from the rack behind him and uncapped the Mason jar. He poured a careful half-inch into each, and the bourbon ran the slow full way that twelve-year bourbon runs. He pushed two glasses across the wood and kept the third for himself.

"Twelve years old. Sixty percent Bradford corn, twenty-eight percent rye, twelve percent malted barley. You're getting it before anybody else in the state."

Jake brought the glass to his nose, swirled, tasted, let the bourbon warm on his tongue, and swallowed without saying anything. It was smooth. The heat settled low and didn't hurry.

Travis grinned. "You like it."

He considered the answer. "It's probably the best bourbon I've ever tasted."

Lila lifted her glass and nosed it and took a small sip. Her eyes closed for a beat, and she nodded once. "Travis, this is wonderful."

"It is, isn't it?" He sat down on the stool opposite them and slapped both hands flat on the cedar. "Man, sophomore year of high school. That's where this goes back to. When did we get old enough to taste twelve-year-old bourbon?"

Jake looked over at Lila. She had brought her glass back to her lips for a second taste, and he waited until she set it down on the cedar. He spoke before he changed his mind. "Remember the fall that year? After homecoming?"

Lila's cheeks turned red and she looked at the mason jar then back at him. "Our first kiss." She looked quickly at Travis then back at Jake and cleared her throat. "We were sixteen. It feels like yesterday. And it feels like forever ago."

Travis had gone very still on the other side of the bar with his fingers spread flat on the cedar. He looked from one of them to the other, then at the Mason jar, and his face split into a wild grin and he slapped the bar top. "We're going to call it First Kiss."

"Travis," Lila said on a gasp.

"Perfect." He pulled his phone out of his back pocket and swiped and tapped. "Sandra. Hold the labels. The ones we approved this morning, all of them. ... I know. ... I know it is. I've got a new name and I want you to draft me some ideas. ... First Kiss. Two words. Capital F, capital K.

Bring me three concepts and a tagline by close of business. ... Thank you, Sandra."

He pocketed the phone and picked up the mason jar, pouring each of them another half inch. "Done."

Jake almost laughed at the audacity of him and didn't. His eyes stayed on Lila instead. She darted a glance at him and looked at his lips like she had the other night. He could tell when she realized it, because she shifted and turned her body slightly away from him. He raised his glass and toasted them. "To yesterday."

Lila tucked the blanket around Mae's knees and slid the mug of black tea onto the side table within reach of her good hand. The window AC cooled the room nicely now that the heat wave had ended. Mae had not said three words since the truck pulled into the gravel.

"You warm enough, Granny Mae?"

"Mm."

She brushed a strand of silver hair off Mae's forehead. "Want me to bring your book over?"

"I'm fine, Sugar. Going to the doctor wore me plum out. Go work. I'll just rest."

Lila bent and kissed the top of Mae's head. Mae smelled like the lilac lotion. The cardiologist had said *she was improving, to not expect her to bounce back like a spring chicken, but then reminded her she wasn't a spring chicken. He told Lila that Mae needed rest, and insisted that she not lift anything heavier than a carton of milk.*

"Holler if you need anything." Mae's eyes were already closed, so Lila straightened and went into the back bedroom that was, as of three days ago, her office.

She powered her laptop on and hit the button on the brand-new printer, then glanced at the white board she'd covered with notes in three colors. She picked up a marker and made a couple of new notes and a notation, then sat down and opened a browser on her computer.

The pre-sale was scheduled to go live at midnight tonight. She'd written the social-media ad copy on Wednesday and queued it through the platform Thursday morning. Six placements, three image variants, two video cuts. The Waller Bourbon logo anchored the corner of every asset, the Whisky Rebellion band photo centered, and the Harper farm sunflower-row backdrop ran behind.

[NEWSPRINT] *Friday, August 29 • Waller Bourbon Presents Whisky Rebellion • Tickets open July 26th.*

She read the copy through. She read it through again. She trimmed two words off the second-image variant, swapped the lone-sunflower image to put the bloom at the end of the row instead of the middle, and bumped the Saturday-six-AM Eastern launch boost to two hundred dollars instead of one fifty. She saved. She scheduled. The platform ticked over to *queued* on all six placements, one after the other, like a row of green lights.

Her email pinged. Three from Ella, one from Katy, one from Bryce Linville's assistant. One from the ticketing platform confirmed the QA preview was clean. One from the insurance carrier confirmed the rider had bound at noon yesterday.

She opened Ella's first.

[TYPEWRITER] *Cassidy live with Hank at eleven. Talking points attached. She's good. Cried in the green room but she's good.*

The next:

[TYPEWRITER] *Hank's producer wants to book her for a six-month touring spot when she's back from the album cycle. We say yes?*

The next:

[TYPEWRITER] *Sending press release in 30 for your approval. Standard post-segment. Nothing scary.*

Lila opened the talking points. They were tight. Ella had run the sheet by Cassidy three times and pulled the phrase *thank you for being honest with me* off the second page after the first practice run because it sounded coached. The lines that remained were Cassidy's actual words, sorted into the order Cassidy would best deliver them. Lila replied to Ella in three lines.

[TYPEWRITER] *Yes to Hank's six-month spot, get the contract memo drafted. Press release approved in advance. Send unless something breaks. Tell Cassidy I am proud of her.*

She sent it then opened Katy's email that contained her approval paperwork for a two-month partial sabbatical and asked her to call before signing. Katy answered on the second ring.

"Good morning. How's Mae?"

"She's tired. But the doc indicated we were out of any weeds." She turned and looked at the white board.

"And you?"

"I'm actually enjoying planning this concert. I've only ever marketed, not planned. It's kind of fun to do something new like this."

"I think it's a brilliant idea." Katy paused. Lila pictured her at her desk that overlooked Music Row. "The good news is you've rarely taken a day off, so you are on paid vacation and not unpaid sabbatical." Lila frowned at the wall. She didn't think she had that many days, but she didn't argue with her. Katy continued. "What do you think it looks like two months from now?"

Her mind went to Jake on her porch with the storm colliding around them. It should be going to Mae, to the farm, to the future that will help her keep the land.

Katy needed the truth from her, not empty promises. "I don't know." She closed her eyes to block out the lists on the whiteboard and the emails on her computer and focused entirely on her boss and friend. "I want to say I'll be raring to come back. But I don't feel that right now." She sighed. "I know that sounds terrible."

"You are the best brand person I have ever worked with. I don't want to lose you entirely. Get through this concert then we'll talk about what our options are."

Lila looked at the whiteboard. *Pre-sale Sat midnight. Concert Aug 29. Bank Sept 15.*

"I wish we could compress distance."

"We have the technology," Katy said quietly. "There are ways you can be in both places. But now is not the time for that conversation. Take the vacation days. Ella is on orders only to email and not text or call unless there's an actual life or death situation."

Lila smiled. "Like Reels from our hottest new artists?"

"Don't get me started." Katy laughed. "Tell your grandmother I'm thinking of her. I'll see you in a month at the concert."

"I can't wait."

The line went quiet.

Lila set the phone down on the desk beside the laptop and looked out the window. The sunflower rows ran thin past the porch. The hawk from Sunday morning was back, working the field.

From the front room Mae's voice came, dry and small. "Lila Grace."

"Yes ma'am?" Lila called back.

"It will work itself out."

Lila closed her eyes for a beat. Mae obviously heard every word of the call.

"Yes, ma'am." She shifted her brain away from the phone call and refocused on her laptop and the to-do list. She had a little less than twelve hours before the ticket sales began.

Chapter 8

Lila lifted the lid off the kettle grill and turned each thigh skin-side down on the grate. The fat hit the coals and popped and sizzled. The aroma made her mouth water. She set the foil wrapped corn on the cooler side of the grill then shut the lid.

"You salt the corn, Sugar?" Mae called through the screen door.

"Yes ma'am. Butter's in the foil too."

A pause from the kitchen. Then the scrape of a chair and Mae's voice, dry. "Charlie. Quit lifting that pot."

"Yes ma'am," Charlie said.

Lila rolled her head on her neck and looked out at the field, imagining the people that would fill it in just a few weeks. Nervous anticipation filled her stomach and she took a sip of cold, crisp wine to still it.

She'd spent the week cleaning Mae's house. Each room got tackled with almost a fury. She was here now. The scrubbing helped her believe it.

Once the house got up to Mae's old standard, she'd started on the yard. So far, she had weeded the porch beds and bought some flowers that would handle the coming autumn weather. She had purchased new paint for the porch railing but hadn't quite made it out here yet to spruce up. One top of the physical labor, she kept up with the administration side of throwing a concert, running ads, and fielding emails from Ella. The week had blurred.

Mae insisted she get her Sunday evenings back. Lila had insisted that she let her do all of the cooking and heavy lifting for at least this week. Charlie had come up the gravel at four-thirty. He had brought a brown paper sack of cherries. He and Mae pitted them and apparently were making a compote that would go over vanilla ice cream. Lila thought about asking to have dessert first.

When she turned back around, Jake stood at the bottom of the porch steps. She took a step back and put a hand over her heart. "I didn't hear you."

He came up the steps and stopped by the grill. "Smells good. I could smell it back by the fence line."

"I love cooking on the grill. I have one on my balcony in Nashville that I use all the time."

He did not move past her toward the screen door. Instead, he lifted the lid of the grill and smelled.

"I haven't seen you all week," she said.

He didn't shift. "You've been busy."

"I have. Long days." She turned the tongs over in her hand. The metal was warm where she had been gripping it. "You could've come over."

"Didn't think you'd want me to."

She stared at him, watching the muscles move under his T-shirt as he lifted the lid back onto the grill. "What does that mean?"

He shrugged. "What do you think?" His tone held no malice but the stoic expression on his face confused her.

She wiped her palms on the sides of her jeans and tried to keep her voice low. "I would have enjoyed winding down some evenings with you." He narrowed his eyes at her. She suddenly felt very foolish. Some part of her thought he'd want time with her, too. She turned to go inside. "Never mind."

His hand closed around her arm above the elbow. "What do you want from me, Lila?"

His grip was not hard. Almost gentle. She could feel the calluses on his hand on the bare skin of her arm.

She looked into his eyes and caught her breath. He'd given nothing away in his face, but it was all there. Finally, she whispered, "My friend."

His eyebrows drew together and he shook his head. "What?"

She pulled her arm from his grip. "My friend, Jake. I want my friend back. I've missed you for a third of my life. I am tired. I am so tired of not having you in my life."

"Whose fault is that?" he asked in a quiet tone.

The last thing she wanted to do was cry in front of him. She blinked back tears. "I know."

A dark look crossed his face. "I don't know what you want me to say."

She raised her chin. "Maybe I'm not going to leave again."

His eyes widened then narrowed again. "Don't say it because you think it'll help."

She did not look away. "I'm not saying it because I think it'll help."

"Then why?"

"Because it's true, Jake. Or it's getting true." She took a breath. "I don't have it figured out yet. But the longer I'm here, the more I want to stay." She stepped closer to him and put a hand on his chest. "I don't want to leave."

He put a hand on her shoulder. The screen door creaked behind him before he could find the word. "Mae sent me this platter for the chicken," Charlie said.

Jake's eyes did not leave her face but he lowered his hand and took a step back.

Lila took the platter from him and smiled a bit too broadly. "Thanks!"

She turned her back on Jake and lifted the lid of the grill. They'd caught the chicken just in time. She loaded one side of the platter with meat and the other with the corn.

"Lila," Jake said. "I don't know..."

"Sugar, you bringing that chicken?" Mae called.

Lila wiped her eyes with the back of her wrist.

"Yes ma'am."

Jake took another step back, then turned and opened the door for her.

Jake sat in his mother's wicker rocker with a sweating bottle of beer in his hand and the dark fields stretched out in front of him. He had the porch light off. Behind him through the screen the kitchen light still burned and moths attacked the window. As the cows silenced, the crickets and frogs and other night creatures ramped up their songs.

He'd missed Sundays with Mae and was relieved that she felt better. But as much as he loved sitting back down at Mae's table, he didn't know if he could handle constantly being in Lila's presence.

He wanted to be there.

He didn't know if he could trust her with his heart again.

Maybe the choice had been made a long time ago, the first time he'd handed his heart over. Maybe she'd had it ever since.

He took a long swallow of beer. He didn't turn his head as the door opened behind him.

"What're you doing up?" Charlie stepped onto the porch with a glass of bourbon. Ice cubes clinked as he sat in the other rocker. "Your cows are early risers, brother. 'Course, you trained them that way, so it's all your fault."

"Couldn't sleep."

For a long minute neither of them spoke. They just listened to the night around them.

Finally, Jake said, "I don't know what to do, Charlie."

Charlie paused in his rocking. "It's a tough one."

After several moments, Jake shot a look at his brother. "That's it? That's your wise wisdom?"

His brother took a sip of his bourbon. "The thing is, Jake, you have never, ever, been with anyone else. She left, you shut down, end of story. She's back here now and you're feeling all the feels, but the truth is you were just waiting for her to come back."

He was right. Jake knew it, but he didn't know if he was willing to admit it outside of his own head. "So I get to just hand her my heart and let her tromp on it again?"

Charlie shrugged. "I don't know what you should do. I've wanted you to be happy my whole life. Getting stuck at eighteen with a younger brother to raise, fifty head of cattle to keep producing, and eighty acres of corn just ready to harvest was a raw deal. But, dude, you rocked it. You made it look effortless." He leaned forward and put his elbows on his knees, cupping the rocks glass in his hands. "It cost you, though. Your future. Your happiness."

Jake pressed the heels of his hands to his eyes. He realized he'd thought he'd gotten over her. Instead, he'd just boxed it all up and put it away in his mind. "She said she doesn't want to leave."

"You believe her?" Charlie asked.

"I want to." He took a sip of beer.

"That's a different question."

Charlie turned the rocker a quarter so he was facing his brother more than the field.

"I'm gonna say this once, and you can ignore it like you ignored my advice about the tractor belt last summer."

"That belt was fine."

"That belt was rotten and you replaced it three weeks later."

Jake didn't argue.

"So you got two roads, brother. One. You let her go, for real this time. You shake her hand, you tell her to take care of Mae, and you don't go down to her porch again. Done. You make peace with eleven more years of the same."

"And two?"

Charlie sat back and took another sip of bourbon. He looked sideways at Jake and the grin came back. "You go get her. You don't sit out here on this porch worrying yourself sick over a beer. Give her a reason to stay."

"Good." Charlie reached over and clapped him once on the shoulder. He stood. He stretched his back until it popped. "I'll help with the milking in the morning."

"Thanks, brother."

"Don't thank me. It might have been terrible advice."

Charlie slapped him on the shoulder and went inside. The kitchen light went off a minute later, and the porch went all the way dark.

Chapter 9

Jake hefted the last pallet onto the stack and squared the corner with his boot. The wood was sun-warmed and splintery against his palms. Behind him the dairy barn cast a long evening shadow over the gravel turn-around. Beyond the barn the corn ran flat and golden until it broke at the fence line. The foot-path through the fields was empty.

He stepped back and took a look at his work. Five pallets, criss-crossed and piled the way his daddy had taught him. A coil of dry brush wedged at the bottom. It ought to burn well.

He'd settled on a bonfire sometime past midnight. It would give them something to do, something to look at, and maybe take them back to high school days; happier days before his parents took their plane to fly to Bowling Green and talk to a craft distiller.

Charlie had helped him drag the pallets out of the equipment shed after the morning milking, then had gone home to get ready for his own day.

He pulled his phone from his back pocket. Seven-forty-seven. The sun was beginning to set.

He blew out a breath now and shoved the phone back in his pocket. He headed into the house and grabbed the bottle of red wine from the Fox Hollow Winery he'd opened and two glasses. When he came outside, she was getting out of her car.

She had on a pair of jeans and a white sleeveless shirt. She reached into the back seat and pulled out a bag. With a grin, she said, "S'mores!"

His chest did the thing it'd been doing for three weeks now. He didn't try to manage it.

He met her at the car. "You look nice," he said.

"Thanks." She tucked her hands behind her. She glanced at the pallets, then back at him. "You build a good bonfire, Bradford."

"I was well trained."

He bent and lit the corner where he'd set the brush. The fire took small at first, blue along the edges, then climbed. Smoke rose straight up in the still evening. The light it threw on her face was a warmer light than the porch light at Mae's.

He stepped back. She stepped back. They stood beside each other and watched the pallets go.

He held the two glasses in one hand and poured them each a small portion, then held one out to her. She took it and said, "You think of everything."

"Not s'mores."

With a snort she said, "True." She held the glass up. "To good days."

He'd pulled the wicker chairs off of the porch and settled into one. She sat next to him. "We have officially sold a thousand tickets," she said.

He raised both eyebrows. "Wow. Well done."

"Yeah. Now to make it go smooth and by the numbers."

"I'm sure with the way you wield a clipboard, that all will go well."

He caught the edge of her smile as she raised the glass to her lips. "Thanks, I think." As she glanced around, she said, "How is everything so different but so much the same?"

With a shrug he said, "It's just easier to leave it." He gestured at the house with his thumb. "I did redo the inside. I loved my mother, but the goose kitchen had to go."

Her giggle lit up the area more than the bonfire. "And your dad's elk themed living room?"

He pressed his lips together and shook his head solemnly. "Had to go, I'm afraid. I much prefer a simpler décor that doesn't require dead animals."

She threw her head back and laughed. "I need to see that."

As she got to her feet he said, "What, now?"

"Sure." She gestured with her hand in a sweeping way. "Lead the way. I can't wait to see how bachelor Jake lives."

He set his glass on the arm of the chair and stood. The fire popped behind them, throwing sparks at the darkening sky.

"All right," he said. "Fair warning. It's not exactly House Beautiful."

"Even better."

He led her up the porch steps, trying to imagine what his house looked like through someone else's eyes. He held the screen door open and she ducked under his arm to go through. They entered the kitchen.

"Oh, Jake."

The pendant lights were on over the island, throwing soft pools of white onto the shining oak butcher block. She turned a slow circle in the middle of the floor, taking in the shiplap above the range, the open shelves with their little parade of houseplants and cookbooks, the farmhouse sink under the window. Her hand went to her mouth.

"I find it hard to miss the geese," she said on a laugh. She crossed to the wall by the doorway, where he'd mounted his grandfather's old hand-crank coffee grinder. She touched the iron handle, careful, the way a person touches something in a museum.

"This is incredible," she whispered.

She ran her fingers along the edge of the butcher block as she came back around the island. The green of the cabinets caught the light. He'd gone back and forth on the color for a week before he'd painted it. "You did this yourself?"

"Most of it. Charlie helped with the tile. Apparently, I'm not to be trusted with grout."

"It's beautiful." She turned to face him, leaned back against the island. "It looks like you."

"Yeah? You think I'm beautiful?"

She had the good sense to blush, but then said, "Yeah. You are."

She was looking at him the way she used to look at him when they were seventeen and the whole world was a porch swing and a long summer. His chest did the thing again, only worse, because the kitchen was small and the light was low and there was nowhere safe to put his eyes.

He cleared his throat. "Come on. Living room's better."

"Okay." He let her lead the way through the doorway. In the middle of the room, she turned a slow circle. "Wow."

He'd painted the walls a soft white and laid down a rug, and he'd kept his grandmother's reading chair by the window because he couldn't make himself part with everything.

"I like it," she said. "It looks like you."

"Yeah?"

"Yeah." She crossed to the bookshelf and ran a finger along the spines. "Still with the Heinlein."

"Some things don't change."

She tilted her head and looked at him over her shoulder. The lamp caught her the way the fire had, bringing out the red in her hair. He was the one who looked away.

She turned then, and her eyes went past him to the little sideboard in the hall. He didn't have to look to know what she was looking at. He'd told himself a hundred times to put it in a drawer, and a hundred times he'd left it right where it was.

She crossed to the frame and picked it up. The two of them at the homecoming bonfire their senior year. Her in his letter jacket. Him looking at her like he'd already lost his mind over her. Which he had.

She didn't say anything for a long moment. She ran a finger over his face on the picture, then put it down. With ease, she set the picture down like it might break, and when she turned to him her eyes were too bright.

"Jake..."

"Come on." He said it before she say anything. "Fire's burning down. We've got s'mores to ruin."

She nodded and followed him out.

The night had gone full dark while they were inside. The fire had settled into a low steady glow, the pallets half-collapsed into a bed of orange. He fished two long sticks out from beside the woodpile and handed her one.

"You were prepared."

He picked up his wine glass. "I had a feeling."

They sat closer this time. He didn't decide to do it. The chairs were where they'd left them, but somehow when she pulled hers in toward the fire it was angled toward his, and his knee brushed hers when he leaned forward, and neither of them moved it back.

She skewered a marshmallow and held it out over the coals. He watched her face instead of the fire. She had a small frown of concentration, as if the fate of the world rested on the marshmallow getting toasted exactly right. "You're staring, Bradford."

"Yeah?" He pierced his own marshmallow with the stick. "Maybe you're the one who's beautiful."

She looked at him for a long moment then back at the fire just as her marshmallow caught flame. She yelped and he laughed and reached over and blew it out for her, and when he looked up she was right there. Closer than he'd realized. The firelight moved across her mouth, and his whole chest was a held breath.

"Jake." Just his name. Soft.

He set down his wine glass.

⊰━━◦◦━━◦◦━━◦⊱

Lila held very still.

Jake's face was so close she could see the small freckle beneath his eye, the one she used to trace with her fingertip a lifetime ago. Her heart thundered in her chest as he lifted his hand. The back of his fingers brushed along her jaw, then slowly cupped her cheek. His thumb settled at her temple where a strand of hair had come loose. His palm was warm and rough from years of farm work.

She wanted this. She had for longer than she'd admit.

Her eyes fluttered closed.

When his lips finally touched hers, the world narrowed to just the gentle pressure of his mouth, the faint taste of wine on his tongue, the way he kissed her like she was something precious he'd been afraid he'd lost forever. It was soft and slow, unhurried.

Oh, she thought, the word blooming warm inside her. There you are.

She lifted her hand and pressed it against his chest, right over his heart. It beat hard and fast beneath her palm, matching her own frantic rhythm. Emboldened, she curled her fingers into his shirt and leaned into him, deepening the kiss just a little.

When he finally eased back, he didn't pull away. His forehead rested gently against hers, his breath warm against her face. For a long moment, they stayed like that — close enough that she could feel the warmth of his skin, the slight tremble in his hand as he brushed his thumb across her cheekbone.

"Hi," he said in a voice so quiet she felt it rather than heard it.

"There you are," she whispered, voicing her thoughts.

He let out a small laugh then kissed her nose and sat back in his chair, holding his hand out. She put hers in his, palm against palm. His thumb moved in circles across her knuckles.

Her mind went back through the years and she settled on that terrible day all those years ago. Her breath hitched and she said, "I'm sorry."

He turned his head and looked at her.

"For everything," she said, flinching a little at the words they'd said to each other, words that could never get unsaid. "We were both hurting. I wish we'd had the maturity to understand that."

He was quiet a long time. Then he said, "It was a long time ago." He brought her knuckles to his mouth and brushed a kiss over them. "We don't have to do all of it tonight," he said.

She rolled her thumb across the back of his hand. "Some of it."

"Some of it." His grip tightened and went easy again.

She sat with that for a long moment. The fire was a steady orange now, the high blaze of the pallets settling into a working bed of coals. She watched a stick at the edge curl in on itself like a question being answered.

He let go of her hand to lean down and feed two pieces of split oak into the bed of coals. Sparks went up. He sat back. He took her hand again like it was a thing he was permitted to do now, and the small permission of it made her chest ache.

The bag of s'mores sat at her feet.

"I think it might be time for dessert," she said.

He looked over at her with a raised eyebrow. "Is that what we're calling it these days?"

She put her head back and laughed, then picked up her stick. "Marshmallows. Chocolate. Cookies."

"Oh, that." He winked and took a stick from her. They impaled their marshmallows in companionable silence. She held hers low to the coals; he held his over a clean flame. Hers went golden-brown all the way around. His caught fire. He blew it out and ate it half-charred, no chocolate or cookie companion.

"Some things don't change," she said.

"Apparently." He refilled their wine glasses and washed his marshmallow down with a sip, then winced like it offended his palate.

She built her s'more with precision, the marshmallow perfectly golden. Graham, chocolate, marshmallow, graham. Pressed. She handed it to him.

"For me?"

"For you. The first one's always for the cook."

He took a bite. He closed his eyes for a second. "Lila Grace."

"That good?"

"Mmm."

She made one for herself. A long, easy quiet settled. She watched a moth find its way around the porch light and away again. The crickets had really gotten started now, and the cicadas under them.

When the fire dropped a second time and the coals settled into the orange glow that meant the night was over, he stood and pulled her up with him. She came easily.

He walked her to her car. Before opening her door, he cupped her face and kissed her once more, slower than the first time. She thought she could just stay right here forever, in his arms, with the night alive all around them. When he eased back, his hand stayed at the side of her neck for one breath longer.

"Good night."

She slipped into her car and he shut the door. She was home within two minutes, but didn't get out right away. She leaned forward and put her head on the steering wheel. The taste of him was still on her lips, the warmth of his hand on her face felt like it lingered. A strange thrill lit up inside her chest at the thought of the next time she'd see Jake. She was going to see him again.

When she finally came in, Mae was in the recliner with the television off. "Long evening," Mae said.

Lila set her purse on the side table. "Yes ma'am."

"Mmhmm." She paused then said, "Sleep well, Sugar."

Lila put her keys on the hook and kissed the top of her grandmother's head. She went up the hall to her room.

Chapter 10

Lila found Jake in the eighth row of the lower field with his hat pulled low and his hand on the back of an ear of corn he'd peeled half open. He was frowning at it.

"Should I be flattered or worried that you came all the way out here?" he asked, without looking up.

"Why, flattered, of course." He glanced at her from under the brim of his cap and then looked back to the corn in his hand. He pressed his thumbnail to a kernel and a small white drop welled out where it broke. "What stage?"

"Late milk. Going to dough by Friday."

She watched the white drop bead and slip down his thumb. "Good?"

"Behind a week. We needed June heat earlier than we got it."

She set her hands on her hips. "How can I help?"

He looked up at her now and shook his head. "How long has it been since you've been in a cornfield?"

She lifted her chin. "It's like riding a bike, I imagine."

He slipped an arm around her waist and pulled her close for a quick kiss, much to her delight. Then he gave her a quick lesson on scouting the corn, reminding her how to do it. As he pulled back another husk and broke a kernel with his thumbnail, he told her it was called the stage. He pointed at the silk. "Check to see if it's brown all the way down or just at the top." He showed her gray leaf spot on a lower leaf, small lesions like cigar smoke, showed her tar spot.

"Got it," she said. She put her hands on her hips. "How many ears do you check?"

"Twenty per acre."

She started a tally. "How many acres?"

"Eighty."

She blinked at him. "How is this not done by a robot?"

"Because the robot doesn't know what tar spot looks like."

"It seems like the robot could learn," she said, then stuck her tongue out at him.

He shook his head and said, "I'd never trust it not to miss something. I need to see myself."

He kept working. She held husks for him and walked in his footprints. The corn was over both their heads, and the air down inside the rows was hotter than the air at the top. It smelled good inside the rows, reminded her of her childhood and helping Jake's mom do this same thing while Jake helped his dad in a different field.

She caught herself enjoying the way the muscles in his forearms moved when he peeled a husk back. She hadn't stopped noticing.

About an hour later, she felt the change in the air as the light darkened. She lifted her face out of the row and looked toward the south.

"Jake."

He looked up too. "We need to move."

He folded his clipboard against his chest, pocketed his pruners, and the wind rattled the top of the corn before he turned. A fat drop hit the brim of his hat.

"Run."

He took her hand at the end of the row, and they cut along the headland and up the slope to the tractor shed at the edge of the field. The rain hit hard before they reached the open door. A wall of water came at them sideways. By the time they crossed the threshold of the shed and skidded in over the concrete, they were soaked through.

They were laughing. He let go of her hand only to push his hat off his head. She shook her arms and water fell like rivulets.

"Welcome to August," he said.

She wiped water out of her eye. The shed smelled of diesel and hot metal and wet hay. The old green tractor sat in the near bay; a newer red tractor in the far one. A workbench ran along the back wall. The rain was loud on the tin roof. The corn beyond the open door was bowing under the water, then springing back. The wind coming through the opening felt cool, and goosebumps rose on her arms.

He went to the workbench and pulled a clean folded shop towel out of a drawer and handed it to her. She used it on her face, then her arms, then her hair. He used his on his face. He pushed his wet hair back with the heel of his hand and left it that way.

She hopped up onto the workbench and swung her ankles. He came to stand close, with one hand on the bench beside her hip but not on her.

"This is the perfect opportunity to ask me a hard question," he said.

"What if I don't have one?"

He shrugged. "Then we wait."

"I have an easy one."

"Try me." His thumb brushed the back of her hand on the bench.

"How is the corn?"

He looked at her. He set the shop towel down. He stepped one step closer.

"The corn is fine. It should be a good year."

She slid down off the workbench onto the concrete in front of him and put her hand on his shirt where her hand had gone before, over his heart, and went up on her toes. He met her there.

She easily wrapped her arms around his neck and leaned into him her mouth finding his. His wet hair was cold under her fingers, and she didn't want to surface.

When he eased back, he kept his forehead at hers and laughed, once, quietly.

"You're bad for my workday."

"I'm very good for your workday."

He pressed his lips against her hair. "That, too."

They waited out the storm. She stayed against his shoulder. He kept one arm around her waist. He told her it would probably be fine—soakers at that stage ran better than wind—but he'd walk the field edge in the morning to know for sure. She told him a story about her assistant Ella ordering four hundred printed banners last fall with the artist's name spelled wrong and not noticing until they'd been delivered to nineteen states. Jake said that was worse than tar spot. She laughed against his collarbone.

The rain stopped in twelve minutes. The smell of wet earth and hot tar and corn-after-rain came in through the shed door. Steam rose off the soybean field across the lane.

He walked her out to her car, parked on the gravel by the road. The sun broke through the clouds and immediately began warming the earth. He held the door for her.

"Come back tomorrow?"

She winked. "We'll see."

Jake set his cap on the seat beside him in the booth and pushed the menu across to Charlie without looking at it. The Hollow Diner hadn't changed its menu in nine years. He didn't need to read it.

"I'm having meatloaf," Charlie said.

"It's Tuesday. Meatloaf is on Wednesday."

Charlie looked at the weekly specials on the back of the menu. "I've been off a day all day. I'll have meatloaf tomorrow, then."

Louise came over with two iced teas and took their orders without writing them down. Meatloaf Special for Charlie. Pot roast for Jake. She walked off.

Jake watched the iced tea sweat down the side of the glass. "Corn's good. Finished scouting it yesterday."

His brother nodded. "May was cooler than normal. Did it throw us off at all?"

He gave a small shrug. "Not enough to be bothered by it."

"Good." He fielded a text and said, "I have help coming to handle the store for harvest."

"We'll know more about when in about two weeks."

"I figured."

Their plates came. They didn't chitchat while they ate, normally, but about halfway through the meal, Charlie asked, "So what's the plan, brother?"

Jake took a deep breath and set his fork down, then leaned back against the bench. "I'm going to wait."

Charlie chewed slow. "Haven't you waited long enough?"

She'd said she didn't want to leave. He believed with the part of him that had been waiting eleven years for her to come back. The rest of him wasn't all the way there yet.

"Because I don't know if she's saying she'll stay because she means it," he said. "Or because she can't leave Mae right now and her mouth is running ahead of her."

Charlie chewed.

"When the land's saved," Jake said, picking his fork back up, "and Mae's on her feet, she'll have no other reason to stay than me. That's when I'll know."

"Hmm," his brother said. "I wonder, why won't you just ask her?" He took a drink of his tea. "It might be good to hear her dive deep and give you an answer."

It might be, he'd admit that. To himself. He just wasn't all the way there. That was allowed.

"If you could see the way she looks at you without the filter of your experience..."

Jake cut him off. "I've waited eleven years, Charlie. I can wait a few more weeks. It gives us a chance to get to know one another again."

Charlie watched him for a long moment. Then he tore a yeast roll in half and buttered one side and ate it. He did not say anything for a while. Then in a gentle voice, he said, "I hope you're not making a mistake."

Jake chuckled and picked up his fork. "Yeah, thanks for all of the relationship advice from the confirmed bachelor of Fox Hollow."

Charlie grinned. "It's the wisdom of youth, older brother."

"Yeah, okay."

Chapter 11

Jake's truck rolled up the gravel. Charlie cracked the passenger door before they'd come to a full stop and rushed up the porch stairs.

The board under Jake's boot at the top step gave the small flex it always gave, the one he'd meant to fix for his daddy and never had. The porch screen had a hand of pot roast in it before he opened it. Onion. Brown bread. Mae's stove on for a long hour.

"Afternoon, Granny Mae," Charlie said as he rushed through the kitchen. Jake reached the door as he said, "Reds are playing."

"It's already on the TV," Mae said, pulling a pot out of the oven.

She looked at him as he shut the door behind him. "You rushing through here, too?"

"I'm not rushing anywhere, Granny Mae." He grinned and walked over to Lila at the sink. Her hair was up. An apron was tied over a yellow shirt. The strings crossed at the small of her back where he could see the bow. She'd left a small scatter of soap on her wrists.

She smiled at him over her shoulder. His pulse climbed. He set a hand at the small of her back. He kissed a bare shoulder. She leaned into it for the smallest second.

"Hi," she said quietly.

He could feel the warm of her skin and the small lift of her breath under his hand.

"Hi."

"That a boy," Mae said, with a small lift in her voice that was as close as Mae came to laughing at him.

He smiled into Lila's shoulder before he stepped back.

"Smells good in here." He leaned over the pot Mae had set on the stovetop. Steam came up. Beef and onion and the long warm of a Sunday.

"Pot roast. Mae walked me through it. Three hours of low and slow." Lila rinsed her hands and dried them on the apron. "Hand me the bowl, will you?"

He handed her the bowl. He'd been handing things to people in this kitchen most of his life, and the small physical fact of handing this bowl to this woman in this room landed in him in a place he hadn't quite been ready for.

He helped her with the salad. She tore lettuce. He sliced cucumber and tomato. Their elbows bumped on the third pass and stayed bumped for an extra beat. Mae stood at the stove with a wooden spoon and worked at the gravy and watched them work and didn't say anything for a while.

"Mmhmm," Mae said eventually.

Charlie hollered something about a curveball from the living room.

The four of them sat down at the scarred oak table with the lazy susan in the middle. Pot roast, mashed potatoes, green beans Mae had snapped that morning, a fresh loaf of bread, a sweating pitcher of iced sweet tea.

Charlie dipped bread in the gravy. "So, yesterday, old man Cline came in for thirty pounds of rye. And somehow, through a conversation I barely remember, I accepted payment in the form of a young goat."

Mae dabbed her napkin to her lips. "Where's the goat now?"

"Well, that's what I'm here to tell you." He took a long drink of tea. "In your hay field."

"My hay field? Do you not have your own field?"

Jake raised an eyebrow at his brother. He was trying not to laugh at the look on Mae's face. "Yeah, Charlie. Do tell."

"Well, we can't very well release goats into the corn, Granny Mae. Remember the debacle of 2015?"

Mae forked a small piece of pot roast and chewed it slow. "Lila Grace can name her."

Lila gasped. "Did you not think we might have enough going on around here, Charlie?" She glared at Jake as if to put the blame on his shoulders, since it was his younger brother's actions that had brought them to this place.

Under the table, the toe of her shoe touched the side of his boot. Once. He kept his face neutral and passed her the rolls.

"You're the one who was upset that your goats died since Christmas and no one told you," Jake said, tongue firmly in cheek. "Let's try to be a little consistent here."

Lila glared at all three of them. Then her face broke into a smile. "Sure," she said. "Gang up on the girl. I hear you. And I'll remember."

Everyone at the table laughed. Charlie finished eating quickly and headed back into the living room with the broadcaster's voice running ahead of him. Jake sat back in his chair. Lila and Mae went on to Mae's sister and a thing about a cousin and a quilt. Lila propped her chin on her hand while Mae talked. Jake enjoyed watching her interaction with her grandmother.

He and Charlie enjoyed coming to Mae's for dinner on Sunday. Mae had always made sure of that.

He'd spent years believing Lila abandoned Mae. He knew Mae didn't feel that way. She wanted Lila happy out in the world, doing what she wanted to be doing. He wanted her here, happy doing what she wanted to be doing.

Maybe that made him selfish. He didn't know. But he did know that sitting here right now, in this kitchen with which he was so familiar, the two women he loved most in the world sat here with him.

Lila wiped her mouth and pushed away from the table. "I made cherry pie," she announced. "Prepare to be amazed."

"Take it out on the porch," Mae said. There was a knowing in her voice that was half tease and half permission. "Enjoy the evening."

Lila fixed Mae's and Charlie's plates and brought Charlie his while Jake cut their two. He held both plates while Lila pushed through the screen door and held it open for him. The door tapped shut behind them.

She settled into a wicker chair and tucked one foot up under her and thanked him when he handed her the pie. He leaned against the porch railing. The evening had gone soft. Cicadas were starting up in the side yard. The corn at the road bend was a dark line against a sky still pale at the top.

He took a bite. Instantly his mouth filled with the tart cherries, a hit of cinnamon, just enough sweet, all wrapped up in a buttery crust. He closed his eyes and chewed slowly. He didn't really want to end this experience.

When he opened them again, Lila was looking up at him.

"Told ya," she said, taking her own bite.

"You certainly did." He savored another bite. He thought, for a second, about saying something he'd been working up to saying. He didn't say it. Instead, he said, "I think I might need to keep you around after all."

She didn't answer right away. She set her fork at the edge of her plate. Then she reached out and brushed her knuckles along the back of his hand on the railing, light and brief. "Well," she said. "That is what I'm trying to work out."

The sound of crashing plates came through the open kitchen window and cut off any reply. Charlie yelled, "Lila!"

Jake ripped the door open hard enough he was surprised he didn't rip it off. Mae lay in a heap on the kitchen floor. He landed on the ground next to her, remembering the last time he'd found her like this.

Lila slid on her knees toward her grandmother, her own phone already at her ear. Her face had almost no color. Jake felt for Mae's pulse. It was there, small and fast. He nodded at Lila.

Charlie reached over and shut off the running sink.

"Granny Mae, can you hear me?" Jake rubbed his knuckle on her chest. She didn't respond.

Lila spoke into the phone. "Yes, ma'am. My grandmother, Mae Harper. The Harper farm on Bowman Mill Road, second house past the cattle gate. She fainted. She's breathing. Yes, ma'am, we'll be here."

Lila's hand moved to Mae's cheek and stayed. She looked up at him for one breath, and Jake saw, in her face, stark fear, the same fear he felt when he found Mae a few weeks ago. He moved his hand and put it down over hers on Mae's wrist and held it there.

⟨——◈——∞——◈——⟩

Mae's hand felt very small in hers. Lila stared at their joined hands and remembered reaching up for Mae to hold her hand as they walked toward the school building the first day of Kindergarten. She tried to remember the last time she held Mae's hand. Was she ten? Eleven. She couldn't remember. But she had never thought of Mae's hand as small before.

The noise from the business in the ER came through the curtain closing off their area. Mae's eyes opened, found her, and closed again.

She leaned closer. "Hi, Granny."

"Hi, Sugar." Mae's voice was a thread.

She bent so Mae would not have to work to hear her. "Sleep. I'm right here."

"Mmhmm."

Lila pressed her thumb against the soft place at the back of Mae's hand. Mae's breath went slow and deepened. The monitor over the bed kept its small green time.

She'd sat in a chair like this before, in a room that hummed like this. The body knew what to do when the mind was somewhere else.

She had not let herself cry yet. But she felt the edge of it. The worst had been sitting right there since she saw Mae go down. Seeing Mae on the floor like that—

A nurse came in. "Doctor should be in soon," she said, checking the IV bag. She held her badge up to the computer, logged in, made a couple of notes, then logged out with her badge. The entire time, Mae slept.

Her own phone buzzed in her hand. Charlie texted into their group thread.

> How is she?

Before she could reply, Jake also texted.

> Do you need anything?

She thumbed back.

> She's sleeping. I'll know more when the doctor's back.

Charlie thumbed-up the message.
She added:

> I don't need anything. Thank you.

Lila looked at her grandmother's face on the pillow and the sliver of color beginning to come back into Mae's lips, and she set the phone on her knee and breathed.

The doctor came in a few minutes later. He pulled the curtain behind him. He was middle-aged, gray at the temples, a soft voice that was used to talking to people who had spent the day being afraid.

"Ms. Harper."

"Lila."

"Lila. I'm Dr. Patel. Your grandmother is stable. Her blood pressure dropped dangerously low this evening, which is why she fainted. We've got her on fluids and we're titrating her medications. We've been in contact with her cardiologist Dr. Owens over in Lexington and we're in agreement she needs to stay with us tonight. We'll have her in a room within the hour."

Lila nodded. Her throat had gone tight without her noticing.

"Was it her heart?"

"Not in the way you're afraid of. The medications she takes for her heart can drop her pressure when they need adjusting. So, we'll be sure to adjust before we send her home."

"Is she — " She tried again. "Is she going to be all right?"

"She is now. She'll be tired tomorrow. Her body's been working hard. We'll watch her overnight, and if her numbers hold through morning, we'll talk about getting her home."

Lila nodded again. "Thank you," she said, relief bringing emotions to the surface. "Truly."

"We'll be back." Dr. Patel touched the foot of the bed once and went out.

Lila immediately texted Jake and Charlie.

> BP dropped. They're adjusting their meds but are going to admit her to keep an eye on. I'll let you know when I know the room number.

Her phone buzzed. Katy.

> What happened?

She brought Katy up to speed in a quick back and forth exchange. Then Katy sent the text that gave her pause.

Tell me what you need.

There was a question that had been sitting at the bottom of her ribcage since she'd come home, and it had decided itself an hour ago somewhere between the kitchen floor and the ambulance. Lila hadn't known until just now that it was decided.

I can't leave her again.

The bubble that meant Katy was typing came up, and stayed up. Lila waited.

Of course not. I'm working a plan. Don't stress about that part.

Mae's voice came up sleepy from the pillow, her eyes not all the way open. "Lila Grace."

"I'm here, Granny."

"They keepin' me?"

Lila pressed her thumb to the back of Mae's hand. "They are."

Mae's eyes closed. "Mmhmm. All right then."

Lila smiled at her grandmother for the first time since the plates had gone down.

An hour later, after getting Mae settled, she texted the group.

Room 314

She heard Jake's boots in the hallway before she saw him. She stood and was halfway across the room before he even came through the door. He immediately grabbed her by the back of her neck and pulled to him, wrapping his arms around her. "That was so scary."

He pressed a kiss to her temple. "I know, sweetheart."

Charlie came in behind him with two paper cups of coffee. He set them on the table and rubbed Mae's leg. "Granny Mae, we're here for you."

Mae didn't open her eyes, but she said, "I know, Sugar," in a slurry voice.

Lila stepped away from Jake. "We should just let her rest. I just wanted you two to see she was alright."

"We can go whenever you're ready," Jake said.

Charlie drove. Lila got into the back without thinking about it. Jake surprised her when he slid into the back seat with her. He took her hand and held it in both of his and looked at the dark window when she looked at hers.

The road from the hospital out to the county was long and dark. The fields were black on both sides. She rested her head on Jake's shoulder and tried to figure out what tomorrow looked like.

Charlie pulled up to the Harper farm at twenty past midnight. He left the engine running and turned around in his seat. "Y'all got it from here?"

"Yes, sir," Jake said.

Charlie's eyes went to her. "Get some rest. She's in good hands."

"Thank you, Charlie."

He nodded.

Jake got out and got her door, then walked her up the porch. The kitchen was the way they had left it. The plates were on the floor where Mae had let them go. A line of gravy went down one cabinet and puddled on the floor.

Lila stood in the doorway and looked at it and suddenly those tears she felt let loose.

It wasn't a pretty cry. It came up out of her like something that had been held under water too long and had finally fought its way to the surface. Her hand went to her mouth and she bent over almost in half. She couldn't get a breath around it.

"Hey. Hey, come here."

Jake's hands were on her arms and then she was against his chest, and he was turning her away from the kitchen back out onto the porch. He kicked the screen door closed behind them with his heel. He didn't let go.

"I've got you."

She tried to say something and couldn't. She pressed her face into his shirt and she cried the way she hadn't let herself cry in the ER. Her fists closed in the cotton of his shirt. He didn't try to shush her. He just held on, one hand flat between her shoulder blades, the other at the back of her head.

"She was just... she was just lying there, and I couldn't... " Her breath broke off her words and a sob tore through her.

"I know, sweetheart."

"Her hand was so *small*."

He made a sound low in his throat, like the words physically hurt him. His arms tightened around her.

She cried until her breath came stuttered hiccups and still he didn't move. The porch boards creaked under his weight when he shifted her a little closer. She could hear his heart through his shirt, steady. Steadying her.

When she could finally talk again, her voice was wrecked.

"I don't know what I'll do if I lose her." She pulled back enough to look up at him. His face was close. Tears filled his eyes. She hadn't expected that, and it almost set her off again. "I shouldn't have left her."

"She wasn't alone," he said. "We love her, too."

Something in her chest broke open a little further. Not the hard break of before. A softer one.

She laid her forehead against his chest again. He rested his chin on the top of her head. For a long minute neither of them moved.

"I have to clean up the kitchen," she said into his shirt.

"I'm cleaning up the kitchen. You're going to go upstairs and take a hot shower and get in bed, and when you come down in the morning you'll be amazed at how clean the kitchen is. That's what's happening."

Her eyes filled again, but it was a different kind of full.

"You have cows."

"I do indeed." He pressed a kiss to the top of her head. "I also have a brother who probably set his alarm because he's cool that way."

She nodded against him. She didn't have the strength to argue with him.

"Thank you." She looked up at him and he cupped her cheek, then pressed a warm kiss to her lips.

"Of course, Lila Grace." He kissed her one more time. "Now, upstairs. Rest. I've got this."

Chapter 12

Jake pressed his thumb on the corner of the vendor map where the porch fan kept lifting it. He held it down until Lila set her coffee mug on the corner and freed him. He flexed his hand and reached for his own mug. The afternoon air was warm, not hot. He looked forward to even cooler weather.

Mae was in her recliner knitting for her knitting club and watching an old western. He wanted to see her up and in her yard, but didn't press her.

"Bless you," Lila said when she set her mug on the corner of the map.

"For the coffee or the corner?"

"Both."

He tipped his cap back. She had shadows under her eyes. When he went out to the milking barn at four, he noticed the kitchen light on. "You sleep last night?"

She shifted a glance at him before looking back at her chart. "Some. I lie down and think of a dozen things I need to remember to do. And when all of that gets resolved, I worry about Mae and check on her." She straightened and put her hands on her hips. "It's just a season. I'm sure I'll be better after the concert."

He took a sip of his coffee. "I'll hold you to that."

She smiled up at him in a way that made his heart rate increase, then went back to her colorful sticky notes and vendor map. "How's it going?"

"I'm playing a board game where I can make up the rules as I go," she said. She shook her head. "I've been to enough music festivals and outdoor concert events through my job that this should be easy. I don't think I have ever given directors of concerts and festivals enough credit."

He thought about what he'd observed in just the last week. "I think most people working on something like this have a team."

"Welcome to the team," she said with a flip of her hair. He laughed and took another sip of coffee.

He settled back on the wicker chair and just enjoyed watching her work the puzzle out. He had a dozen chores he needed to do, but for now he was content to enjoy his coffee break and her.

The crunch of tires on gravel interrupted his thoughts. He looked up as a black SUV nosed up the drive.

"You expecting anybody?" he asked.

"Nope."

The SUV stopped at the bottom of the porch steps. Jake recognized Chase Whitfield, current mayoral candidate and land developer. He'd moved here four years ago from Los Angeles. He wore a pale blue oxford shirt with the sleeves rolled to the elbow. The driver's door had a large square magnet on it that said, "WHITFIELD FOR

FOX HOLLOW." The muscles in his neck tightened. He knew the man wasn't here on campaign business.

"Lila. Glad I caught you."

Lila did not stand. She set her marker on the table. "Mr. Whitfield."

"Chase, please." He came up the steps with a practiced smile and his hand already out. "And Jake. Good to see you on a porch instead of a tractor."

"Mr. Whitfield." Jake did not stand either.

"Chase," Whitfield said. "Mind if I take a minute?"

"A minute," Lila said.

She did not invite him to sit. Whitfield sat anyway. Jake registered the move. Jake set his own mug down as he straightened.

"How is Mae?"

"Resting."

"I was sorry to hear about Sunday. Nora wanted to bring food. I told her to give you a few days."

Jake stayed silent, letting Lila take this lead. This was her grandmother's property, her business. However, if he felt like he needed to intervene to protect these women, he certainly would not hesitate.

"That was kind of her," Lila said.

"Mae's tougher than the rest of us."

The smell of Whitfield's cologne drifted toward Jake and he kept his face from scrunching up against the smell.

"She is."

Whitfield glanced at the map. "How's the concert coming?"

"We sold out in a week. Kind of exciting, really."

"I hear good things about you from my friends in Nashville. That's an extraordinary outcome for a such a short build. You should be very proud."

She smiled, but Jake noticed it did not meet her eyes. "Thank you."

Whitfield tilted his head. "Look. I know the timing of this is awkward. I sent the offer letter back in July. With everything you've been navigating, I haven't wanted to push. I respect the family piece of this." His voice came down half a register. "I just wanted to come by in person. The offer stands. Two-forty. I can't go any higher. Mae would keep the house inside of an acre and lives here for the rest of her life with no rent and no fuss. The lower acres and the road frontage are what we're interested in."

Jake heard the number again. Two-forty. Mae could pay off any debt and would be set up financially indefinitely. He knew what taking it would cost.

Lila shook her head. "No, thank you."

Whitfield's smile didn't move. "I appreciate you hearing me out."

"I hear you. The answer is no. Mae and I aren't selling any part of the farm. I know you have a vision for it. I respect that. I've spent seven years writing brand decks. I can read yours from across a room." She gave him a small, neutral smile. "It's a good deck. This just isn't the farm for you."

Whitfield looked at him as if to appeal to him man-to-man. Jake raised an eyebrow as if to ask, "Say, what?" Then Whitfield looked back to her. The smile held. "I want to be careful here. I don't want you to feel pressured. Especially this week. I just don't want you to make a decision in a hospital corridor."

"I'm not in a hospital corridor."

"No, ma'am, you're not."

Jake felt his shoulders go a quarter-inch tighter. "She gave you an answer."

It came out low and even and surprised him a little for being out at all. Whitfield did not miss it. Something passed across the man's face. A small recalibration. The smile came back.

"Of course." Whitfield stood and brushed the front of his shirt again. "I won't take any more of your morning. You've got a show to run." He looked at the vendor map and tapped it lightly with two fingers. "I'll see you at the concert."

"I hope you enjoy it."

He paused at the top of the steps and turned back. His voice was easy this time. "If anything changes, Lila, my number's on the letter."

"Understood."

He drove back down the drive as carefully as he had come up it. The dust rose behind him and settled slowly back over the gravel. Jake's hand moved from the chair to the back of her neck and squeezed. He didn't say anything for a moment.

"You good?" he asked.

"I'm good." She reached over and kissed him softly, then leaned her forehead against his.

Lila let the wine wake up against her tongue and watched the light on the square soften. The oaks along the sidewalk had thrown their shade across the brick by six and were just now letting it go. Two tables over, a couple was finishing a slice of cheese. The patio of Hollowbrook Cellars held the warm of the day even as the streetlights came on along the curb. She hadn't felt easy in a long time.

Jake came back from the counter with a beer in a glass that fogged a little where his hand had been. He set it on the table almost silently and dropped into the chair across from her. Gone was the usual jeans and T-shirt with a UK baseball cap. Instead, he wore a pair of khaki slacks and a button-down shirt that brought out the blue in his hazel eyes.

"What?"

"Nothing." He took a swallow. "You."

She smiled into the rim of her glass. The candle in the center of the table was encased in a glass holder that protected the flame from the breeze. Between them sat a little wooden board with two cheeses she didn't know by name, smoked turkey rolled into scrolls, olives, and crackers fanned around the edge. They had ordered the small, and the small was plenty.

"I appreciate Charlie sitting with Mae. It means I can relax completely." She ran her finger over the rim of her wineglass.

"It's a hardship for him to watch football with her," Jake said in a dry voice. His mouth twitched. "I'm sure you'll owe him a favor."

She laughed and reached for an olive. "He's a good man."

"I raised him well. Taught him everything I know."

She laughed again, then set down her wine and propped her chin in her hand, studying Jake's face in the light of the square. She searched for the teenage boy she'd known inside the man sitting across from her. He took a sip of beer, and she watched his hand curl around the glass, the shift of muscle in his forearm, and remembered how those hands felt on her skin, how those arms felt around her.

It occurred to her that she had fallen in love with him again. She had probably never stopped.

She didn't say it. She picked up an olive and ate it slowly, and the truth settled in her chest. She'd hold it for now. Maybe she'd lay it out later, or let him make the first move. Instead, she pulled out her phone. "I have something to show you."

"Yeah?"

She tapped through to her email. The proof had come in from the Nashville printer that afternoon. She turned the phone toward him.

It was a heather-gray T-shirt, photographed flat on a backdrop. Across the front, in a clean lowercase serif: *sunflowers and fox hollow* Below it, smaller, the date and FRIDAY in caps. On the back was a single line-drawn sunflower, petals a little uneven on purpose, with the words *The Waller Bourbon Sunflower Concert* in a circle around it.

Jake studied it. "I like that. Well done." Out of nowhere, emotion filled her chest. He looked up. "Why are you tearing up?"

"I'm not." She was. "I just can't believe all of this is coming together. It shouldn't be. There should have been a dozen things gone wrong."

He slid the phone back to her. "You're quite incredible."

She took a sip of wine to take a pause and get herself under control. "I ordered twelve hundred. Plus a hundred for the volunteers." She sat back. "Katy is picking them up from the wholesaler on her way into town Thursday. Saved me the shipping."

He reached across and took her hand on top of the table. She felt the rough places on his palm where she had spent the last few weeks learning the shape. His fingers were warm, strong. She would never get tired of them. She turned her hand until their palms met.

A black sedan slid up to the curb across the square. The polish on it caught Lila's eye against the matte of the brick. She watched Mayor Caldwell get out dressed in a tuxedo.

A woman came down the wrought-iron stairs that ran up the side of Sweet Mercy. She was in a sage-green dress that caught the streetlight in the same way the silver at the mayor's temples had. She held the skirt up with one hand. The mayor took her hand at the bottom step and watched her face.

"That's a pretty dress," she said.

Jake stared at her and ran his eyes down her dress, taking in the lilac print covered in little white flowers. "Pretty everything."

She gasped and laughed. "Jake!" she said on a breath.

"Just observing."

Out of nowhere, she decided to tell him how she felt. Forget waiting. They'd waited long enough.

"Jake." He reached for an olive and raised an eyebrow, waiting. Her phone buzzed against the wooden table. She didn't check it, but it grounded her, kept her from saying something she might have wished she had waited to say. "I'm really glad we're here."

The smile on his face was warm, sincere. "Me too, Lila Grace." He reached across the table and turned her hand palm-up. She let him.

Chapter 13

"East three feet."

Jake shouted it over the auger and pointed at the chalk square Lila had laid in white that morning. The foreman made a circle in the air with his finger, the engine wound down, and the bit lifted out of the loose dirt with a soft sucking sound.

The foreman waved him over. "Show me again, Mr. Bradford."

"Jake's fine." He walked the line with his boot. "Stage skirt runs here. Food trucks back of the line. We need the pole clear of the cable run. East three feet puts you past it."

The foreman jotted something on his clipboard. "Ms. Harper walked us through it at seven this morning. We had it down. Then she moved a vendor square."

That didn't surprise him. "You should be good to go now."

"All right." The foreman waved his bucket man up. "East three. Get on it."

Jake stepped back and pulled the brim of his cap lower. The Kentucky August heat sat on his shoulders and burned the back of his neck. The field was busy in three places at once. The Kentucky Utilities crew worked on installing the temporary power pole, two carpenters worked on building the stage, and Lila had hired a landscaping crew to work a riding mower out by the gate, stripping the parking lanes one swathe at a time. The work made a clean noise.

He walked the chalk line down to where Lila had marked the row of vendor squares. Each square was the size of a ten-by-ten tent and laid in fresh white powder. The lines were bright. She had been at it since the dew burned off.

He spotted her down the row, on her knees, sighting along a tape measure with one eye closed. She wore jeans and the heather-gray T-shirt the printer had made up. Her hair was pulled back and there was chalk on her forearm. She frowned at the tape, nodded once, stood up. She popped the chalker onto its wheels, grabbed the long handle, and started backing down the next line.

He made his way down toward her with a stake under his arm and a rubber mallet in his hand. He needed her guidance about the cable run before he committed it. He was trying to figure out what point he got so invested in this concert. But he knew, of course. He loved her.

Watching her work with intensity to save her grandmother's farm added to the weight of holding in his feelings another second. He'd decided in the milking parlor at five that morning: today he would tell her.

She was backing down the line with her chalker, working the wheels in a long easy arc. She looked over her shoulder once, corrected, kept going. She didn't look again. He stayed still, certain she'd seen him. Apparently, she had not because she backed straight into him and the chalker clipped the toe of his boot. She gave a soft cry and turned, half-laughing, her hand coming up to brace against his chest before she even saw it was him.

"Jake."

"Eyes on the road, Harper."

"Eyes on the line." She laughed and pushed his chest lightly with her palm. The palm stayed there. "I would not run a parking lane into your boot."

"Could've fooled me."

She looked up at him. Her cheeks were flushed from the sun and the work, and there was a smudge of white chalk across the bridge of her nose. He thought he had never seen anything prettier. He thought a lot of things he didn't generally say.

He put his hand at the back of her head and bent and kissed her. It was warm and unhurried. Her hand pressed flatter against his shirt over his heart. He felt her smile under his mouth before they parted.

"Hi," she said.

"Hi."

She tipped her forehead toward his and her breath was warm against his chin. He wanted to back up half a step and look at her face and say it. He had the whole sentence built in his mind.

Lila Grace, I love you. Always have. I want you to stay.

He drew a breath.

Her phone buzzed against the back pocket of her jeans. She made a small sound of apology and reached for it, and he caught her wrist without thinking and then he let it go. The phone came up between them. She glanced at the screen.

Her whole face changed.

It was not a bad change. She lit up, smiled.

"It's Cole Banks," she said. She looked up at Jake quick. "Give me a sec."

She stepped back from him and swiped the screen and pressed the phone to her ear and walked four paces toward the open field.

"Hey, you. Where are you?"

He couldn't hear what came back through the earpiece. He could hear her voice though.

"You're here? Today? I thought tomorrow."

She put a hand on her hip and laughed. The laugh carried.

"Well. That's a surprise. No, no, that's fine. That's wonderful."

He turned around and walked back to his stake. He set it. He drove it with the mallet, two strikes, clean and even. He picked up another and walked it down the line. With each strike he thanked whatever providence kept him from saying those words out loud. The humiliation...His heart twisted painfully and he thought of the things he had neglected at his farm in deference to her concert.

Behind him she said, "Of course I want to see you. Yes. Yes, tonight works."

The foreman caught Jake's eye from the pole truck. Jake lifted two fingers, and the foreman nodded and went back to his man on the bucket. The auger started up again. Good. The auger covered some of it.

He drove the next stake. He picked up another, walked it down the line, drove it clean. By the time he was on the third one his shoulder started to burn, and he was glad for the burn because it was a clean, ordinary thing his body could do without his help. He kept his back to her on purpose for one stake, and turned a quarter for the next, and made himself face her again.

She was pacing in a small circle in the cut grass. Her free hand kept moving, tracing the air as she talked and laughed. The light came down on her shoulders soft and yellow. She was happy.

She closed the call and dropped the phone back into her pocket and walked toward him fast and a little sheepish, the chalker squeaking behind her on its wheels because she'd forgotten she was towing it.

"That was Cole," she said.

"Heard that."

"He's in town. Drove in early. Said he wanted to be settled before the bus and the gear and the road managers showed up tomorrow." She pressed her lips together, then released them. Her face was still flushed. "I'm going to grab a coffee with him after we wrap here. Just to say hi."

"All right."

"Jake." Her hand came up to his shirt the way it had ten minutes ago, but she put it there with a question this time. "We broke up months ago. You know that."

"I know." He held the mallet against his hip.

"Do you want to come with me?"

He barked a laugh. "In a word, no."

She watched him, searching his face. He kept his face open and easy, even smiled a little, because she needed him to.

"Mark your spots, Harper. We're losing daylight."

She pressed up on her toes and kissed his cheek and went back to her chalker with her shoulders set.

He turned to his stake. He drove it. He moved on to the next.

He wasn't heartbroken. He noticed that. He turned it over with the mallet in his hand. The feeling was something sharper—more like remembering.

What had he expected? He turned that over too. He had stood on this field for three weeks watching her run a sold-out concert with a phone in her back pocket and the rest of her old life on the other end of it.

She would go. She'd always go. The joy she'd shown at the phone call, of someone from the Nashville world coming into this clean space, had settled it.

He'd spent more than a decade learning how to lose her once. He could do it again. He'd started already.

Lila let her car idle at the stop sign on Maple and watched the courthouse clock change from six to six-oh-one. The light on the square was the long gold of August evening. From the corner she could see the white awning of the coffee shop, the wrought-iron tables under it, and Cole at one of them with a folded newspaper and a cup in front of him.

She pulled into the spot behind a black sedan and shut off the engine. For a second she sat with her hands on the wheel.

She was excited. That was the truth of it. She'd been excited since the call had come in that afternoon. It was the excitement born from anticipation of something she hadn't noticed was missing until it showed up.

Part of it was that Cole being here meant the concert was actually going to happen. All of it. The bus, the gear, the crowd. He'd walked into Fox Hollow ahead of every truck and rigging case and road manager, and that meant the rest of it was real.

The other part was harder to name and easier to feel. Cole had been her friend before he'd been anything else, and her life used to be full of those. Friends. People. A dozen communication threads at once. Coffee with someone every morning, drinks with someone else after work. Now her life was Mae and Jake and Charlie. She loved Mae and Jake and Charlie, and she really didn't want it to be anyone else. But the idea of a face from her old world, a person she could be casually glad to see, made her smile against the dashboard.

She caught the smile, shook her head once at herself, and got out of the car.

The work-day was bleeding off the storefronts as she crossed the square. A man in a Rotary polo was lowering the courthouse flag. Two women were closing up the bookshop on the far corner. The breeze had cooled the brick by a degree.

Cole saw her before she got to the table and stood up. He hadn't put on the rockstar for this. He wore a simple plaid shirt with a white tee underneath and jeans. His blonde hair had the beginning of salt at his temples, and he wore a couple of days of beard.

"Lila."

"You beat the bus," she said.

"By a day." His mouth lifted on one side. "I'm told I'm insufferable when I can't be the first one in the room."

She laughed, surprised at how easy the laugh was. He pulled her into a brief, one-armed hug. He smelled exactly the same. She set her bag on the chair across from him and sat.

"Can I get you something?"

"I'll get it." She caught the eye of the girl behind the counter, held up two fingers, and pointed at Cole's cup. The girl nodded.

He lifted his folded newspaper. "Did you know your local paper has a column called 'Around the Square This Week'? I read it cover to cover."

"That column is older than I am."

"That tracks."

She sat back and looked at him in the setting light. She'd known him for two and a half years. She coordinated his launch, worked closely with him for months. A year later, he asked her out and she had readily agreed because she liked him. She didn't know what made her think that his enjoyment of after concert parties and all the things groupies offered would go away because they were supposed to be in a committed relationship.

"Before we get into the catch-up, there's something I want to say." Cole set both hands flat on the table. "I'm honored you asked me to do this, and I want you to know I don't take it lightly."

The girl from the counter set a coffee in front of her and hesitated just a fraction of a second longer than necessary, giving Cole a little half smile. Lila almost shook her head at the predictability of it.

"You were the first person I thought of."

"I know we have history." He pressed his lips together for a second. "You could've called any of half a dozen guys and not picked the one with our specific complications. I just wanted to say it on the front end, so you knew I knew."

She nodded once and felt her shoulders come down. It was the right thing for him to say. It was the thing she hadn't known she needed him to say until he was saying it.

"Thank you," she said.

"Of course."

They sat with the coffee. She let a beat go past, then leaned her elbows on the table.

"While we're doing the front-end conversation."

"Have at it."

"I want to make sure you and I are on the same page about what this is." She kept her voice warm. "You're doing me a tremendous favor. You are literally saving the farm. Like some after school feel good special. I will be the most grateful woman in Kentucky on Saturday morning. But this isn't a thing where we're easing back into anything else. I want that clear."

Cole watched her steady and took a swallow of his coffee.

"Lila. I drove down a day ahead of my band so I could shake your hand and tell you I was honored. The concert is for your grandmother's farm. That's why I'm here. Not to win you back."

"Okay." She believed him. Mostly. She set down her coffee and reached for his hand on the table. She gave it a squeeze and let go.

She lifted the lid of her coffee and watched the steam curl off it. "Tell me about Bryce. Is he still scared of his own assistant?"

"Petrified."

She laughed again. She hadn't laughed twice in a string with anyone but Jake in three weeks

They drank their coffee. Cole told her about the support act and an unnamed road manager he was already lobbying to fire. She gave him the parking-lane numbers and the projected gate. The work between them lifted onto the table the way it used to, professional and easy.

After a while she looked at the courthouse clock and stood.

"I have a six a.m."

"Of course you do."

He stood too and hugged her again, the same one-armed careful hug. She took her bag and stepped back.

"You good on your own?" she asked.

He shot a quick glance at the cashier in the coffee shop then back at her. "Of course."

She almost shook her head, again, at predictability. "See you tomorrow," she said.

"See you tomorrow."

She walked the half-block to her car in the late afternoon light. With her hand on the door, she stopped before she pulled it open. This had been good. It was good to see a friend. To laugh and relax. But it also affirmed what she already knew. Her heart and head belonged in Fox Hollow, not Nashville anymore.

Chapter 14

Jake pushed Mae's screen door open with his shoulder and let it close gentle behind him.

The smell of toast and coffee from the morning lingered. The auger had started up out in the field a half hour back. The bucket truck was on its second pole now, replacing a guy wire the KU foreman had flagged at sunup. About thirty hours from now, people would be filling that field out there.

"Mae?"

"In here."

She was in the recliner with her reading glasses on the end of her nose and a Louis L'Amour open across her lap. She looked up over the rims.

He came all the way into the room. "I came to check on you."

"I figured."

He took his cap off and held it. He didn't sit. He didn't want to stay. "All this racket bothering you?"

"All what racket?" She tipped her head toward the open window. The auger was steady at it. "That's not racket, Jake. That's a sold-out concert getting itself born."

"Lila's idea of a Tuesday."

"Lila's idea of a Tuesday is twelve things at once and the right answer for each of them." She closed the book on her finger. "I'm fine, son. Right where I want to be."

"All right." He turned the cap a quarter in his hands. "You want to come over to my place for the day? Get out of the noise. I can run you over in twenty minutes, sit you on my porch where it's quiet, fetch you back at supper."

She looked at him a long moment. "That is the kindest offer I've had this week." Her mouth tipped, and for half a second, he saw Lila in it. "But I'm staying right here. My granddaughter is putting on this show. I'm enjoying the running soundtrack."

"All right."

"Sit a minute."

He almost said no on reflex. "Got things to do."

"Sit anyway."

He sat. He turned the cap on his knee.

Her gaze stayed steady on him. She had never asked him about Lila in all these years. She just...knew.

"You'll eat lunch," she said finally. "There's chicken salad in the fridge. I made you each a plate."

"Yes, ma'am."

She nodded. He stood. He set the cap back on his head and bent and kissed her on the top of her silver head.

"Go on, then."

He left her with her book and headed into the kitchen. He opened the door then shut it because the thought of food held no appeal. Maybe he should find Lila and tell her what bothered him. If he could voice it properly, she might be able to alleviate his concerns, make him believe she intended to stay.

A diesel horn sounded on the gravel out front, big and tour-bus deep, and an engine settled into idle.

Jake stepped onto the porch.

The bus was forty feet of glossy black with WHISKY REBELLION painted across the side in gold script. Two SUVs and a box truck had pulled in behind it. Doors were already opening. A man in a ball cap climbed down out of the bus and walked toward the field with the easy stride of a road manager.

Lila was already coming up from the vendor area. Her hair was pulled back and she had a yellow legal pad braced against her hip. She met the manager halfway. He stuck a hand out. She took it and pointed past him and Jake heard her voice carry across the dooryard.

"The barn is yours. Hay loft was cleared yesterday. Cases stack along the south wall. Power's run if you need it."

The manager nodded and turned to wave his crew in. Lila was already moving, hand up to shade her eyes, scanning the line of vehicles for whatever came next.

Cole came down the steps of the bus. Jake's teeth clenched.

He had on a faded gray T-shirt and jeans with sunglasses pushed back in his hair. He spotted Lila across the gravel and his face lit up. He covered the ground in five long strides. His arm went around her waist and lifted her clean off the ground and swung her in a half-circle. The legal pad hit the gravel.

"There's my girl!"

Jake turned around. He went back through the screen door and crossed the kitchen, going into the front room. Mae looked up. Whatever she saw she didn't ask about.

"Going to my place," he said. "I'll be back this afternoon."

"All right, son."

"Charlie's coming by at two. If I'm not back, send him to the south gate."

"I'll send him."

He went out the back door. He walked the long way around the house to the truck so he didn't pass the bus. He got in and rolled out of Mae's drive without looking at the field.

He wasn't heartbroken. He had known that since yesterday, out on the field, and it hadn't changed. He was angry.

The man had lifted her off the ground like his hands belonged on her, the one he called his girl.

That was the anger. He turned it over the whole drive and it stayed the same.

A piece of it was embarrassment. He could name that too. He had stood on Mae's porch for half a second thinking he should go see Lila and voice what he was thinking, make her hear his worries.

He thought about Lila for a count of three and then forced his mind to chores and work. Work was what he had.

His piece of the concert was done. He had told her he would see her concert through and he would. He would walk the field with her tomorrow morning if she needed him to walk it. Friday night he would stand wherever she pointed, and Saturday he would lift what wanted lifting.

That was all he had left in him.

He pulled into his own drive.

The cows were down at the south fence where they had been at sunup. The barn doors were still open from the morning chores. The corner post by the gate had been leaning a week and he had told himself he would get to it after the concert. He could get to it now.

Lila marked the last corner of the last vendor square and pushed up off her knees, and that was when she heard the diesel horn.

She stretched her back and shaded her eyes. The bus was already turning into the gravel drive, glossy black with WHISKY REBELLION painted in gold across the side, a box truck and two SUVs trailing behind it. She tipped the chalker onto its wheels and started up the row toward the house. Her stomach was empty. The chicken salad she had been thinking about for the last forty minutes was waiting in Mae's fridge. She would eat after she pointed the road manager at the barn.

The manager, Ian Barclay, came down the steps of the bus first, in a ball cap with a clipboard. She met him halfway across the gravel.

"The barn is yours."

Ian nodded and turned to wave his crew in. Cole was off the bus a beat later, and before she could step back he had her off her feet.

"There's my girl!"

Her boots hit the gravel and the legal pad hit it with them. She was already turning, already pushing, both hands flat against his chest and shoving him back a clean step.

"Cole."

"Hey, easy."

She put a finger up close enough that he had to back his chin up. She could smell bourbon on his breath. "You may never grab me like that again." She didn't lower the finger.

"Lila, I..."

"And I am most certainly not your girl."

He blinked. The half-grin he had come down the bus steps with came off his face.

She turned on her heel before he could put it back on. Ian had stopped halfway to the barn with a road case in his hand, very intently not looking at her.

"You good?" she asked him. "Need anything else from me right now?"

He shook his head. "No, ma'am. We've got it from here."

"Find me if you do."

She picked up her legal pad off the gravel without looking at Cole, walked up the porch steps, and let the screen door slap shut behind her, harder than it deserved.

Mae was watching from the recliner with her glasses on the end of her nose and the Louis L'Amour open in her lap.

"Well," Mae said.

"Indeed." Her hands trembled, and her pulse beat hard at the base of her throat. Lila set the legal pad down on the kitchen counter and pressed both her hands flat against it. Her palms were pink where she had hit Cole's chest. She breathed in through her nose and out through her mouth twice.

"Maybe you ought to go find Jake," Mae said.

Lila looked over her shoulder. Mae had her glasses up off her nose now and her thumb in her book. She wasn't asking. She was telling.

"I'm not leaving you with a busload of strangers in the yard."

"They aren't strangers. The man with the clipboard is doing his job and the boys are carrying cases."

"They're strangers, Mae."

Mae closed the book on her thumb. "Charlie's coming by at two."

"It isn't two."

She crossed the kitchen and pulled out her phone. She thumbed to Jake's contact and pressed the call. The line rang four times and went to his voicemail. She hung up without leaving a message. She stood with the phone in her hand and looked at it.

A knock came at the front door. She went, expecting the road manager.

Cole was on the porch with his sunglasses off and his hands in his pockets. He had pulled his face together. He didn't try to smile at her this time.

"Can we talk?"

"On the porch."

She didn't open the screen door wider than her own shoulder. She stepped out and let it close behind her, which put her between Cole and the house, between Cole and Mae.

"I owe you an apology."

"You definitely do."

He put his hands in his jeans pockets and looked at her. "Waller poured a few at the distillery this morning. He's generous with what's in the rickhouse. I had two over my line. I shouldn't have grabbed you and I shouldn't have called you that."

"That's not a defense, Cole."

"I know it." He pressed his lips together and looked at the porch boards. "Lila. I'm sorry."

"Okay."

"For everything. I love you. I do. I always will."

He said it so casually. A year ago it might have hit her in the gut. Today it didn't. It was just a sentence Cole said when his afternoon had gone sideways and he had bourbon in his blood.

"You don't love me, Cole."

"I do."

"You really don't." She kept her voice steady. "I'm the one woman in your sphere who can tell you no, and that has always been the appeal. The minute I stopped being the no, you'd be shopping the room again." She paused for a beat. "Ask me how I know."

He looked at her for a long second. Then he laughed. It was a short, drunk-edged laugh and it surprised both of them.

"You're right." He scrubbed a hand down his face. "I'm sorry."

"I know."

He looked up from the porch boards. "Concert's still on?"

"Of course. Why wouldn't it be?"

"Okay." He turned and went down the porch steps and back toward the bus, hands in his pockets, not looking back. She watched him reach the gravel before she turned around and went back inside. Mae had her glasses on the end of her nose again and her thumb in her book. She had not moved.

"I'm hungry," Lila said, the anger dissipating as rapidly as it had come. She knew Cole was sorry. She had dealt with handsy musicians more than she'd care to lay out.

"Chicken salad in the fridge. Like I told Jake five minutes ago."

"Jake?" She left the kitchen and went into the front room. "Jake wasn't here?"

"Sure he was. He left when that bus came." Mae cleared her throat and took a sip of her ice water. "Tore outa here, even."

Lila closed her eyes and made herself picture what he had seen from the porch, then think it through. If he'd seen her push Cole back, he certainly would have intervened. He must have just left when he saw the bus pull in.

⟨——◗◖——∞——◗◖——⟩

The Old Tobacco Barn at Sycamore Ridge had been a burley barn until the Greene family ran out of children to work it. They'd hung white market lights from the rafters, sanded the plank floor, and hauled in farm tables long enough to seat thirty. Brides booked it eighteen months out for a ridiculous amount of money considering that it was a barn. Tonight it was holding a road crew and a band and Lila's catered dinner.

She had her hand on a galvanized tub of iced soda cans when the front sliding door rolled back, and Charlie came in with Mae on his arm.

"Charlie." She crossed to him. "I thought Jake was bringing her."

"Change of plan."

"Where is he?"

Charlie set Mae's tote down on the bench beside her and helped her sit. "He's not coming tonight."

"Why not?"

He looked at her steady. He had Jake's eyes. "I think you ought to ask him that yourself."

Her stomach dropped half an inch.

The catering captain caught her eye across the room with a question about the chafing dishes. The fiddle player was asking Cole's manager Bryce something near the bar. Cole leaned against a post with a glass of something amber, and a girl from the catering crew had stopped to laugh at whatever he had just said.

She put it aside. She would have to. She put a hand on Charlie's arm. "You're staying, right?"

"I am."

She crossed the barn at a pace that would let her catch the captain before the chafing dish became a problem, and on her way she passed Cole. He had a fresh glass and the catering girl was now pointing at his sunglasses and laughing. Lila put her hand on Bryce's elbow as she went by him.

"Get him under control."

Bryce winced. "Trying."

"Try harder. He's drunk and he's sliding."

"On it."

She kept walking. The chafing dish was fine. The captain wanted to ask her about replenishment timing. She answered it. She moved on.

Across the barn Waller had a circle of three road-crew men around him and was telling them about the difference between a sour mash and a sweet mash, and Cole had drifted from his post toward Waller's circle with his amber glass in his hand. Bryce was on his way over. Lila let Bryce do his job.

Mae and Charlie sat at a table, eating from plates full of food. She grabbed two bottles of water and a lemon sparkling water and carried them over. "Would you like anything other than water, Charlie?"

"No. That's good."

She slid into the chair across from them and looked at the crowd. She enjoyed the sounds of laughter, conversation, music. But she wished Jake was sitting here with her. She made herself stay in her seat instead of leaving her party for his house. She honestly had to table that until after tomorrow.

Chapter 15

Jake pulled the claw off Number Forty-One and swung the milker back into its dock.

The vacuum pump kept its steady hum behind him. He hit the post-dip and watched Forty-One duck her head out from under the swing arm and walk herself out toward the exit gate. He had started at five. Charlie had come up out of the rye operation half an hour later. They were down to the last six head.

He set the milker on the next cow. The pulsator picked up its rhythm. He moved down the line. He hardly noticed the smell of iodine in his nose and how it mingled with the scent of the wet concrete of the wash-down floor under his boots. The bulk tank cooler kicked on out in the room beyond and the parlor lights flickered with it for half a second.

Charlie was on the back side of the pit, washing teats on the next pair. Paper towel in one hand. Iodine cup in the other.

Jake post-dipped, cracked the gate, sent the cow on. Charlie sent his. The sun was up over the corn line now.

Yellow light came in through the open south end of the parlor and lay flat across the rubber mats.

"What time do you think it will get hopping over there?" Charlie asked.

"Who knows," Jake said. "I think shuttles start at two. Concert's at seven."

Charlie set his cow loose and slapped her gently on the rump. "You missed a good dinner last night. Lila knows how to put on a spread."

Jake didn't look up. He set the next milker. He waited for the beat where Charlie usually picked up the running joke about the rye-trade goat, or the next dumb thing he'd accepted as payment. Charlie wiped his hands on the rag at his belt and stood there with the towel.

"You going to keep doing this?"

"What?" Jake set the milker then put the post-dip cup back in its bracket and turned to him. Charlie had their dad's stubborn line in his jaw. "I'm working, Charlie."

"That's not what I'm talking about." Charlie didn't smile.

"Then you're going to have to be more direct."

"All right." Charlie hung the towel on the rail. "Quit being stupid. Go see her."

Jake leaned his hip on the rail and looked at his brother. He didn't say anything. Charlie didn't move. The pulsator kept its rhythm.

"Tomorrow's as good a day as any."

Charlie shook his head and turned to fetch the next pair. Jake watched him from where he stood. He expected the conversation to be over. But when Charlie pulled a heifer through the gate and got her in the stall, he said, "I have seen more life in you the last three weeks than I have seen in ten years."

Jake looked at the floor between his boots.

"And if you're letting her go over a misunderstanding, brother, you are a fool."

His jaw set. The image of Cole's arms going around Lila's waist in such a familiar way --.

"You don't know what you're talking about, Charlie. You weren't there. You didn't see what I saw."

"That so?" Charlie didn't move. "What did you see?"

He didn't want to say it out loud. "She obviously loves Cole. That's what I saw."

Charlie stood with the rag on the rail and didn't say anything for a beat. Then he laughed. He laughed with his head tipped back and the back of his wrist against his eye. His shoulders moved with it. The vacuum pump kept on. Jake didn't move but he began to feel the low burn of anger.

"Something funny?" he asked through gritted teeth.

Charlie wiped at his eye one more time. "I might not have seen what you saw yesterday, but I'm guessing you didn't see the whole picture because I was there last night."

"What about last night?"

Charlie wiped his hands on the rag again. "That woman ran the room last night. From the moment she walked in to the moment I left. She had the catering captain on her left and the road manager on her right. A fifty people were moved where she pointed them. The fiddle player asked her permission before he took a break. The Nashville Lila I have been hearing about for years, in the flesh, in front of the both of us."

The pulsator cycled. Jake glared at his brother, waiting for the punchline, and realized he was going to make him ask. "And?"

"Cole was leaning on a post with a glass of bourbon, and a girl from the catering crew was all over him. She wasn't being subtle about it." Charlie shook his head once. "He was nowhere near your powerhouse. Every time he drifted over toward her, somebody needed her and she turned, and he wound up talking to the back of her head."

Jake stared at his brother.

Charlie put the rag back through his belt. "I guarantee you that woman is not leaving here. And if something does call her back to Nashville, like some knucklehead who threw away his second chance without even thinking twice, Cole Banks is not the man she is leaving with." He spat on the ground. "Even if he came in here thinking he was."

They made eye contact a beat longer. Then he picked the towel up off the rail and slapped it against his thigh and went to fetch the next pair. He didn't look back.

Lila ticked the last connection on the cable run from the temp pole, then turned for the porch and saw Jake coming up the gravel drive. Her shoulders, tight since the kettle came on at five-thirty, pulled tighter.She kept her feet where they were. The legal pad went against her hip.

He came across the gravel slow and even. The vendor trucks were due at noon and he was going to help her confirm that every spot that requested it had electricity. He was two hours late.

She had needed him on the south field at seven. She hadn't realized it until he wasn't there, and then she'd realized it about the dinner the night before too. She'd wanted him there. She needed him there. He'd ghosted her and she didn't even know why.

She did know that this concert was the only reason she was up and functioning this morning. The concert was what would save Mae's farm.

He came up to within five feet of her and stopped. "We should talk."

The words hit her in the throat and for a moment she couldn't speak. Now? Did he not think her plate might be full? She had been planning to deal with this after the concert. She had said as much to herself in the kitchen at five-thirty when the kettle was on and he hadn't replied to her texts. Of course, he didn't know that.

She kept her face the same and met his eyes.

"I have nothing to talk about, Jake." She looked at her watch without registering the time on it. "I have things to do."

"I know you do." He shifted his hat on his head. "I'm asking for five minutes. Less than that."

"You had yesterday to ask me for five minutes. You had a phone."

"I know it."

"I called you, Jake." Her voice came out steadier than it felt. "Right after I put Cole back on his heels and sent him to the bus. You didn't pick up."

His throat moved. "I didn't have the phone on me."

"No. You were in your truck, leaving."

He didn't deny it. A breath went out of her she hadn't meant to let go.

"Yesterday was supposed to be a good day, Jake." She paused, took another breath, let it out through her nose. "You and I have been working really hard and I — " She shook her head once. "You took it from me. From us, really."

"Lila." He took a half step forward. She put her hand up and he stopped where he was. "I saw him pull you in his arms and swing you around. I've been taking it apart in my head ever since, and I came here to—"

"Do you trust me, Jake?"

She hadn't meant to ask him that. The question came up on its own and landed in the gravel between them before she could pull it back.

"What?"

"You either trust me or you don't. I thought we were building something the last few weeks. But that kind of something doesn't work if the trust isn't there."

She set her teeth in the back of her mouth and held them there.

"Lila, that's not—"

"Because if you had, Jake, you would have anticipated that I shoved him away and told him not to touch me. You would have even defended me against a man accosting me." She blinked back tears. She didn't have time for emotion this morning. "But you assumed something about me that wasn't true and you left."

He opened his mouth and shut it.

"You saw what you expected to see and you left. And then you didn't come to dinner. And then you weren't out here like we planned at seven this morning."

"Lila –"

"No," she spat. "You don't get to do this right now. You had a chance. You could have called me. Texted me." She waved a hand in the air. "Send a smoke signal." She pointed a finger at him. "Or, I know, shown up."

Her phone buzzed at her hip. She let it ring twice while she made the decision whether she would answer it. She turned her back on Jake and put the phone to her ear. "This is Lila."

"Good morning," Bryce said. "Confirming one for sound check."

She tipped her head back. A hawk rode a column of air over Jake's lower field, wings held wide and still.

"Yes, one. You said your crew would be here at eleven?"

"Yes."

"I've set up a green room in the barn. And there will be a meal served at five."

"Did you get the food requirements?"

"Yes. I'm hesitant to provide bourbon after what I've observed the last couple of days."

Bryce paused before speaking. "I'm afraid it's a contingency."

She closed her eyes. "I'll make sure it's there, Bryce. But as someone who's been in this business as long as you have, you and I both know this is going to end badly if you don't get a handle on him."

"Another time, Lila. We have other things going on today."

Her mouth pulled into a closed-lipped smile. "Fair. See you at one."

She disconnected and turned around. Jake still stood there.

"If you're going to be on this farm today, you're going to be useful. Right now, you are making this day harder, not easier, and I do not have the minutes in me to make it easier for you. I am asking you to hear that. Please."

He nodded once, slow. The words cost him something—she could see that—and he took them and didn't say anything.

Chapter 16

Jake fed the last run of cable along the back lip of the stage and tied it off where the riser would cover it.

The plywood smelled raw under the August sun. He'd finished the vendor booths at twelve-thirty. He walked back across the field and put himself wherever the Whisky Rebellion road crew told him to be. They needed a longer extension and a hand muscling a monitor wedge into place. He'd said yes to both.

The sun sat almost straight overhead now. His shirt stuck to his back. He pulled his hat off and dragged his wrist across his forehead before putting it back on. The sound check was in fifteen minutes. The kid running the snake crossed the deck for the sixth time, tablet in one hand and a roll of gaff tape in the other. The fiddle player and the steel guitar man sat at the side of the stage tuning out of open instrument cases. Behind the stage, the bus was parked where Bryce had pulled it in. The vendor row down the south side of the drive had four trucks and two tents up so far.

A car came up the gravel. Jake kept an eye on it in case he needed to turn around another enthusiastic groupie. A small silver hatchback with Tennessee plates pulled up short of the porch and stopped.

He didn't know the woman who got out. She wore jeans and a soft denim jacket that was wrong for the heat with a leather tote on one shoulder. She stood by the open door of her car looking at the porch.

The screen door banged and Lila came down the steps two at a time. He hadn't seen her move that fast in years. She crossed the drive at a half-run. Her arms were already opening. The woman dropped her keys into her tote and met her on the gravel.

They held each other a long beat. Lila pulled back. She said something Jake couldn't hear, and her hand went to her mouth. Her shoulders shook. Then she hugged the woman again.

He looked down at the cable and went back to tying it off. The two of them went up the porch steps and the screen door banged once behind them.

He imagined Katy had arrived. Lila had been excited she was coming, enthusiastic even. Jake went back to work setting the cable. The deck crew muscled a second wedge into place at the lip and he watched them get it seated. The tightness across the top of his chest that had been there since his conversation with Lila tightened. There was a time he'd have met Katy in the drive and walked into the house with them.

He pulled the next coil up out of its bin. Several minutes later, the screen door banged again.

He looked up because he couldn't help looking up. Lila came across the gravel with the woman beside her. The other woman walked half a step behind and listened while Lila spoke and pointed. For some reason, they headed straight toward him.

He set the cable down and wiped his hand on the leg of his jeans. They came up to the foot of the stage and stopped.

"Jake." Lila's voice was even. "This is Katy. Katy, this is Jake Bradford."

She stayed three feet back and put her hands behind her back.

Katy stepped forward and held out her hand. He took it and she closed her other hand over the back of his. Her grip was warm and steady. "It's so good to finally meet you." Her smile was the real article. "I've been pestering her about you for weeks. I told her on the phone Monday I was going to come up here this weekend whether she wanted me or not, just so you and I could meet in person."

Jake's throat moved. "Pleased to meet you."

Katy's eyes held his a beat longer. "I'm very glad we're going to be in each other's lives."

"Katy." Lila's voice was quiet and clean. "Let me show you the green room before sound check."

"Of course." Katy let go of Jake's hand. "Lead on."

Lila didn't look at him. She turned. Katy turned with her, and the two of them walked off across the gravel toward the barn. Lila's voice picked up the businesslike tone she'd been using on the phone with Bryce. He heard her say *one o'clock* and *bourbon*, and then they were too far across the drive for the words to come back to him.

Jake stood at the foot of the stage with one hand on the cable he'd been about to set.

A breath came up out of him. He hadn't known he was holding it. The tightness across the top of his chest unhooked itself a notch, and the next breath went deeper than the last one had in days.

She was staying.

Lila came around the side of the house with a paper cup of iced tea sweating cold in her hand and saw the field full at last.

The sun had dropped behind the corn line a quarter hour ago. The sky was still doing the long gold-and-rose work of an August evening in Kentucky. The string lights crisscrossing over the lawn had come on a song before. Twelve hundred faces sat or stood in the soft gloom past the barn, packed into the south lawn and spilling into the first cut rows of the field. The buses that brought them up from town and from the lots down by the lower acres were parked nose-out in three neat lines beside the access lane.

The vendor row down the south side of the drive had stretched into something she'd only seen in renderings on her laptop screen. The Whisky Rebellion merch tent at the head of the row was three deep at the table. She could see the heather-gray T-shirts moving across the counter as fast as the kid behind it could hand them. Two booths down was her sunflower stand. "Sunflowers and Fox Hollow", lowercase serif on the chest. Line-drawn sunflower on the back. The line at her booth was as long as the Whisky Rebellion line, and one of Bryce's interns was running the register with both hands. Every shirt off that table was a few more dollars against the number the bank had put on the farm.

Past the merch was the food row. The barbecue truck from over in Versailles had its smoker running on a low blue flame. Manny's taco truck had a paper sign taped to the order window that read "NO CARNE ASADA, POLLO ONLY".The lemonade trailer beside him had a hand-printed sign in chalk paint announcing "peach today".

The Waller booth was the one she couldn't stop looking at. Travis's crew had hauled a portable building up from the distillery that morning on a flatbed and dropped it into place beside the lemonade trailer. From the outside it was a plain white shed with WALLER BOURBON painted across the side in barn-red letters. From the inside, when you stepped through the door, you were standing in a tasting room cut from oak staves. The walls were lined with reclaimed barrel wood that smelled like char and caramel even from the gravel. A long shelf inside held bourbon candles in squat amber jars. The labels were the ones she'd helped sign off on three weeks back. Travis himself was behind the little counter in a clean denim shirt with the sleeves rolled, talking with a woman in a sundress about the difference between a wheated mash and a high-rye, laughing the slap-the-bar laugh she remembered from high school.

Lila let herself stand in the gravel and look at the whole row for a beat. Then she turned for the porch.

The deputy at the foot of the porch stairs unfolded out of his camp chair when he saw her coming. Wes Hadley had been a year ahead of her in school. He'd been the kid who carried trays for the lunch ladies without being asked. He stood now in jeans and a soft button-down with the cuffs rolled to his elbows, his belt riding without the duty rig. Only the way he kept the porch steps in his peripheral vision gave him away.

"Lila Grace." His voice was low and easy. "This sure is something."

"Wes." She tipped her cup at him. "Thank you for coming. You didn't have to spend your night off in a camp chair."

"Granny Mae's house isn't getting trampled on my watch." He smiled the small Wes Hadley smile she remembered. "I can see the concert just fine."

"Has anybody come up?"

"Two folks asking where the bathrooms were. One man wanting to know if Cole would take pictures after. I sent him to Bryce." He nodded once toward the deck. "Mae's been holding court since seven."

"I'm sure she has."

She went up the porch steps. Mae was in the rocker she'd always been in. A blue cotton shawl was across her shoulders against the air that would cool out of the field once the sun set proper. She had her silver hair pinned back the way she pinned it for company, and her reading glasses were folded on the small table beside her with a paperback Louis L'Amour spine-up next to them. She wasn't reading. She was watching the stage.

"There you are, Lila Grace." Mae didn't take her eyes off the stage. "I was about to send Wes up to fetch you."

"I had to walk the row." Lila settled into the rocker beside her. The porch boards thrummed under her feet with the bass coming up through the gravel and the foundation timber. "A part of me wondered if we'd fit twelve hundred."

"Looks good to me." Mae smiled over at her and reached over and put her hand on Lila's wrist. The hand had the weight of a small bird. She left it there a beat and took it back. "You've done a thing here, Lila-girl."

"We've done a thing here, Granny Mae."

The band moved into the second song before Mae could say anything to that. Cole's voice rose out of the speakers and washed over the field, the porch, and the rooftops of the buses parked down on the lower acres. He'd pulled the song off the second album — the one that charted regional last winter. She'd argued in three meetings for track three instead of track seven but executives with C's in their titles had overridden her. The crowd recognized it at the chorus.A cheer rolled through them, and the roar of it pressed up into her chest.The bass player worked a slow walking line under the guitar. The steel sat back in the mix exactly where it belonged. Whisky Rebellion sounded tight tonight.

They'd come on the stage at seven sharp. Now they played the room like they were made to do it.

Lila let her head go back against the slats of the rocker.

The contract Katy had handed her at three that afternoon sat on the kitchen counter inside. She hadn't read every word of it. She didn't have to. Katy had told her the gist over a hurried supper, while Lila stood at the kitchen sink eating leftover BBQ chicken sandwiches. She had enough of an idea of what it said.

She would have the opportunity to work three week remote, with one week in Nashville every month. The label would cover her travel expenses. She'd have to come down for the special-event days for the label, and for the launch weeks of any artist she ran point on.

If she had written it down, she couldn't have come up with a better plan. Even if she couldn't work things out with Jake, she still needed to stay for Mae. She couldn't leave her and risk something else happening when no one was around.

She listened to two more verses with her eyes half on the stage and half on the field and let that sit.

She looked at the empty chair next to her and suddenly longed for Jake to fill the space. That was his spot. Since yesterday, she kept finding the thought there before she'd asked for it. He'd been present all day, taking care of details, handling people, running interference – just like they'd planned when scoping what the work would look like.

Now he was absent. Again. But this time it was her own doing. She'd been very clear, and she'd been right. Right didn't keep her from being sad about it, though. She'd seen him across the south field at seven on cable duty. He was somewhere in the back of the parlor when the meal went out at five. The road crew had him for the second half of the afternoon, and she'd heard him through the back of the kitchen window when she'd gone out the back door. He'd done what she'd asked. He'd also stayed off the porch.

The song ended on a long fiddle note. The crowd took a big breath together and shouted as the steel guitar man stepped up to the mic for the bridge into the next song. Lila clapped with her hand on her thigh because her other hand had her tea. The porch boards picked up the count-off. Cole laughed something into the mic about Mae Harper's farm and the way the corn smelled at sundown, and the field made the low warm noise of a crowd that had decided to like everything.

Halfway through the next song, Wes Hadley stood up.

Lila felt him before she saw him. She turned her head in the direction Wes looked and saw a figure walking. She recognized Jake's stride.

He crossed the gravel toward the porch. He stopped at the foot of the steps and shook Wes's hand. Wes said something low Lila didn't catch, and Jake nodded once, then Wes sat back down.

Jake came up the steps.

Mae didn't turn her head, but she lifted the hand that wasn't under the shawl and patted the porch swing on the other side of Lila. "Sit down, son."

Jake sat down on the porch swing. He didn't look at Lila and Lila didn't look at him. But she could feel the heat from his body. The porch boards thrummed under all three of them on the next bass kick.

Something inside her, something that had been pulled thin and tight since seven that morning, eased.

She relaxed and listened to the band.

They played the song from the first album the Lexington station had picked up four years ago. The slow one came next, the one Cole had written about a girl from Nashville who turned out to be from a town four hours east. The crowd sang the chorus back at him with the words he'd written, and Cole grinned at the mic and let them. After that came a Hank Williams cover the steel guitar man had requested at sound check, and the steel sat all the way out in front of the mix for it. Near the end of the set they hit the new single Lila had run point on the launch of in March, and the response on it was bigger than the response on the slow one.

Cole was a front man who could make a crowd of twelve hundred people in a sunflower field feel like a private back-porch jam, and he did it for the whole set. He told stories between songs that sounded like he was telling them for the first time. He laughed when he flubbed a lyric and the crowd laughed with him. The band stayed tight under him; the bass locked so clean with the kick that Lila stopped hearing them as separate instruments, the steel bending a note at the end of "Tallahatchie" that she felt somewhere in her chest.

Everything flowed exactly the way she'd laid it out in the weeks leading up to this.

The encore ended on a long note from the fiddle that the crowd held into a roar, and the lights came up in the field. Cole took the bow he took at the end of every show, both hands on the mic stand and his head down. The crowd didn't stop cheering. He waved. The band waved. Cole said, "Thank you Fox Hollow! Thank you Mae Harper!" into the mic before they walked off.

The applause didn't stop for a long time.

Lila let it run. She let the field do its work. She watched the kid at the front-of-house console bring the house lights up in stages so the crowd could find their way back to the gravel without anyone tripping. The buses started their engines down by the lower acres in a low diesel rumble that ran under the cheering.

Then she stood up.

"I'm going to the barn to make sure the green room's set for the after-show," she said to Mae. "If anybody needs anything, that's where I'll be."

"Go on, Sugar."

Jake stood up with her without saying anything. Wes nodded at them both from the camp chair. Lila came down the porch steps with Jake half a step behind her and crossed the gravel toward the barn in the cooling dark, threading between the last of the crowd that had peeled off toward the buses and the ones still drifting toward the merch row for one more T-shirt.

The barn door was open the way she'd left it at six and she nodded to the security that stood guard. Inside, the green room she'd set up that morning was still mostly intact. The table along the back wall held the water bottles in a galvanized tub. The platters of cornbread, fried chicken, and pickles the catering crew had laid out before the meal were down to crumbs and bones. The hay bales stacked along the side wall made seating. The standing lamps Bryce had asked for so the band could see what they were eating were on. The Whisky Rebellion crew had been through and would come back through, but for the moment the barn was empty.

The string lights from the field didn't reach inside. The noise of a thousand people talking mingled with the bass thrum from the buses pulling out reached in through the open door and ran along the planks of the floor.

Lila walked to the table along the back wall and set her empty cup down on it.

When she turned around, Jake stood close enough that she had to look up at him to meet his eyes. "I have something I need to say," he said. The barn had gone quiet.

Chapter 17

Her hair smelled like peaches like it did when they were seventeen. Some small, cracked thing in Jake's chest split wider, and he knew if he didn't say it now, right now, he never would.

"I love you, Lila Grace."

It came out rougher than he'd meant. Quieter.

Her eyes widened and her breath hitched. He wanted to reach out and touch her, but he kept his hands at his sides.

"I never stopped." The words tumbled now. "I'm not going to. There has never been anyone else for me, Lila. There never will be."

"Jake—"

"Let me finish." His voice came out firmer than he felt. He softened it. "Please. I let you finish this morning. It's my turn."

She closed her mouth. Her eyes filled with tears, but they stayed on his. Waiting.

He cleared his throat. "I didn't want this." The admission scraped coming up. "God help me, Lila, I didn't want to let us burn again. I had every intention of keeping my distance. Most of me figured you'd settle Mae and sell up and go back to Nashville where you belong, and I'd be standing in the drive watching your taillights again." His throat worked around the image. "I had a plan for that day. I had it all mapped out, how I was gonna survive it."

He dragged in a breath. "I lost you the first time because I let your hurt feed mine, and I let mine come back at you twice as mean. We chewed each other up, Lila Grace. Both of us. And I have spent a third of my life hating myself for every word I said that day." His jaw locked around the memory. He forced it loose. "I am not doing that to you again. To us."

Voices sounded outside the barn. He paused, made sure no one was coming in, then continued.

"Somewhere in these last weeks, watching you be incredible, beautiful you, I realized how much I need you in my life. But the truth is, I had this mental preparation of how I would survive you leaving again. It drove me yesterday, made me react. That was wrong."

He held her eyes, and his heart was beating so hard he could feel it in his fingertips.

"I love you and I want you. However you'll have me. Wherever you are. I'll figure the rest out."

She didn't move.

Finally, she said, "I love you, Jake Bradford."

He reached back and caught the edge of the table. How many seconds of his life had he waited for those words to cross her lips again? He didn't dare move. He just stood there and let those four words rearrange every dark corner he'd built inside himself over the years.

"I didn't realize how I had never stopped," she said, "until I was in your arms again."

She pulled in a breath, and he watched her chest rise with it, watched her gather herself. He found himself breathing with her.

"I thought what I wanted was in Nashville. I built a life there believing that." Her green eyes didn't leave his. "Until I almost lost Mae. And until I had you again."

She closed the space between them.

Her hands came up to his face—cool palms against the rough of his jaw. He closed his eyes, savoring the feel of her skin on his. Then she came up on her toes. And she kissed him.

Her mouth was warm, soft. His hand slid into the soft weight of her hair, cradled the back of her head, and he kissed her back.

She pulled back an inch. Her forehead stayed against his. Her breath was warm on his lips. Before he could move, she let go of him and stepped back.

"I love you." Her voice was quiet. "And we are not going to be together if you cannot trust me."

He held still. How could this conversation have a but?

"I'm not selling the farm. I'm not leaving Mae. I'm not leaving Fox Hollow." She said each one like she was laying down cards she'd already decided he couldn't take from her. "But the work I am good at is in Nashville."

More voices passed the doorway of the barn and she looked over his shoulder as if assuring they were still alone. "I will keep working for the label, spending at least a week every month there. I'll be on planes. There will be men who lean too close, who get handsy. There will be cameras in my face."

Every sentence pulled his stomach tighter. He knew where she was going. He knew, and he deserved it.

"Cole is not the exception, Jake." Her eyes held his, and there was no condemnation in them. Just unflinching honesty. "He is most of the men I work with."

His jaw set on its own. A muscle jumped in his cheek.

She raised an eyebrow and he knew she could see the anger resurface.

"I love you, Jake. However, I will not spend every month of my life under the weight of you wondering what or whom I might be doing."

His throat closed.

"I would rather have a broken heart than live like that."

She reached up and cupped his face right where the muscle in his jaw moved. "You need to reconcile my life with yours, or we cannot have a life." She held his eyes, searched his face. A bootfall sounded on the barn floor and she looked over his shoulder again. "I'm asking you to think about that. Seriously. Search your heart." She pressed one more quick kiss to his lips and he inhaled the peach smell. "We should talk more tomorrow after all of this is gone."

She stepped backward and sideways, then walked to the front of the barn. "Y'all, that was incredible!"

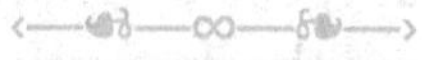

Lila let herself in through Jake's back door and stopped on the mat to listen.

Low jazz came through the Bluetooth speaker propped on the windowsill. The scent of garlic and soy sauce filled the room. Jake stood at the island, brushing a marinade on some skewered chicken. He wore a red T-shirt and a pair of jeans.

Her stomach had been knotted up the whole walk here.

"Hey," he said as she came in. "Just in time."

"It smells good."

He set the tray aside and washed his hands. "Charlie dated a cook for about a month. She was a master with marinades."

She crossed to the island and slid onto a stool. She linked her fingers together to keep from fidgeting. "Can I help?"

He shook his head. "All done. Meat on a stick and a salad. What more could you want?"

The smile helped loosen some of her nerves.

He leaned a hip against the counter behind him. "How're you?"

"Tired." She smiled. "I slept until ten. I felt like I could have slept longer but I went ahead and got up." She rolled her shoulders. "For some reason, my body is sore."

"You ate stress for weeks. I'm sure that has something to do with it." He walked around the island and came up behind her. Suddenly, his thumbs were pressing into the exact spot her shoulders ached.

She held in the moan and closed her eyes, leaning her head forward. "I'll give you exactly an hour to quit doing that."

He chuckled. "Were you going to go to the festival today?"

"Mmm," she said when his hands shifted up her neck. "Um, no. I think I've had enough crowds for now."

"Word on the street, according to my brother, is a rousing success of the concert. People are already asking who you're bringing in next year."

A burst of pride flowed through her. "That's awesome."

He released her muscles then stepped back and rested his hip on the island. "I'm really proud of you. However it turns out."

She sat back in the stool. "I did some preliminary numbers this morning. After everything is paid out, we cleared enough to cover the bank note."

His eyes brightened as a grin covered his face. "Well done, you."

She shook her head. "Not just me. You worked as hard as I did."

"No, actually, I didn't." He waved his hand in the direction of Mae's farm. "Your idea, your groundwork. I just provided muscle."

He moved to the cabinet and pulled two stemless glasses out and set them on the island in front of her. He reached for the bottle of red wine he'd had breathing on the counter. He poured them each a splash.

"To Mae's farm," he said, handing her glass to her and holding his up.

Her breath hitched and emotion flooded her chest, bringing tears to her eyes. She was clearly still exhausted. "To Mae's farm."

The wine tasted good. She closed her eyes, appreciating the dry flavor on her tongue. When she opened them again, she caught him watching her. She had been working up to this question all morning. It came out softer than she had planned.

"Are we going to be celebrating anything else, Jake?"

He didn't answer right away.

He set the wine down on the counter. He looked at his hand on the glass for a beat, then looked up at her.

"I couldn't sleep last night," he said. "Thinking about our conversation last night."

Her stomach tightened. She held the glass with both hands in her lap.

"After I milked the cows this morning, I watched the sun come up and went through it piece by piece." He rolled his shoulders once, like the work was still settling in them. "I'll tell you what I came to. You tell me if it's enough."

She ran a tongue over her top lip. "Okay."

"The problem wasn't Cole." He said it flat. "The problem was I saw him, and I went straight to the certainty I already had about you leaving. I had it ready since the first week you came home, because I figured if I was prepared, it wouldn't cut me the way the first one did."

She set her glass down on the island, slow. A tear slid down her cheek.

"I was going to leave first because then I would be in charge of what hurt in the end." His jaw worked. "Bright idea."

"Jake —"

"Please, hear me out."

She closed her mouth.

"I trust you." He said so plainly. She slid out of the stool and stood in front of him. "I do. The piece I didn't trust was me. I didn't trust I'd survive you leaving a second time, so I was rehearsing it. Every day. In the back of my head. I don't think I realized how much I was ready for it until I reacted." His lips twitched in a small smile. "Reacted badly, I'll add."

"Yes," she said, smiling even as another tear slipped down her cheek.

He drew a breath and let it out. "Your job has you surrounded with stars, working with them, interacting with them. You'll be in green rooms and on planes and in front of cameras, and there'll be some Cole-shaped man sometimes." His mouth moved at the corner. "I know who you are. I know how you make me feel. I know how much I love you and want to be with you. I do trust you."

She couldn't speak for a moment. Then she made herself look up.

"So," he said as he picked his wine back up. "Are we going to be celebrating anything else?"

"Yeah." Her voice went soft. "Yeah, Jake. I think we are."

She set her glass on the island and slid out of the stool. He didn't resist as she took the glass from him and stepped close enough to see the flecks of gold in his eyes. His hand came up to the side of her face, his rough palm resting on her jaw. He searched her face, then lowered his mouth and kissed her. She stood on her toes and wrapped her arms around his neck. She could feel his heart racing along with hers as he pulled her closer.

He slowly broke the kiss, then pulled back an inch and looked down at her. She cupped his face with her hands and said, "I love you."

He held her eyes. "I want to marry you. I want to raise a family with you. And whatever direction your work goes, I want to be the man you come home to."

She tried to say his name. It came out as a half-breath. He brushed a thumb under her eye, catching the tears there.

"Yes," she said through a small laugh that broke up under the tears. She had been so afraid walking here, and now he was offering her an entire world. "Yes."

His arms went around her and lifted her half off the floor. He held her there.

He didn't let go.

Epilogue

Mae's fingers were warm at the back of Lila's neck. She fastened the last small pearl button at the top of the lace and let her hand rest there a moment longer than the work needed. Lila felt her own held breath let go.

"There," Mae said. "There you go, Lila Grace."

The mirror in the small bridal room at Waller Distillery reflected the two of them, Lila in the white lace dress Mae had sewn herself and Mae in a lavender suit and her hair set fresh that morning. The dress had cap sleeves, lace at the collarbone that lay flat, and the skirt fell full from the waist with a lace edged train.

Lila turned to face her grandmother and didn't know what to say.

"Don't you cry," Mae said. "Your makeup is perfect as is."

Lila laughed. The laugh broke a little under the tears she was already not crying.

Mae reached up and tucked a sunflower into the soft coil at the nape of Lila's neck. The petals brushed the side of Lila's jaw.

"Cut from the back row this morning," Mae said.

"Granny."

"Mm-hm?"

"I love you."

Mae patted her cheek. "I love you, too, Sugar." She stepped back and looked at her, head tilted. "All right. Let's go marry that boy."

They walked out together. The bridal-room door opened onto the back hallway of the Barrell Room. The hallway smelled of old oak and bourbon, the long sweet note that drifted toward Mae's farm whenever the wind shifted west. Lila had smelled it her whole life. Today it smelled like home.

Katy waited at the threshold in cream silk with a small bouquet of bound sunflower stems in her hand. She looked at Lila and put a hand to her mouth.

"Stop it," Lila said. "You stop that or we will all of us be a mess."

"I am a professional," Katy said. "I do not get emotional on the job."

"You're not on the job."

"That's the trouble." Katy laughed and hugged her one-armed so the bouquet would not crush. She stepped back and shook her hands out at her sides like a singer about to walk onstage.

The doors at the end of the hall stood open. Beyond them Lila could see the long shape of the Barrell Room, dark wood walls and iron trusses overhead, white lights strung from beam to beam. The tall garage doors at the far end were rolled wide to the patio and the late-October sun on the Kentucky countryside. Rows of folding chairs ran down both sides of the polished floor with an aisle of cream linen between them. At the front, against the open doors, three men stood waiting.

Charlie in a navy suit, his hand at his cuff. Travis Waller behind a small lectern with a leather folder.

And Jake.

He wore a navy suit and a cream tie with a sunflower at his lapel. When he saw her, the set of his shoulders changed. She could not wait to get to the end of the aisle.

The string trio at the side of the room slid into the soft figure that was their cue. Mae took Lila's right arm at the elbow. She did not lean on her, exactly. She did not need to. But she put her hand there and kept it there.

"You ready, Lila-girl?"

"Yes, ma'am."

"Good. Don't run."

They walked past friends, coworkers, extended family. Lila kept her eyes straight ahead, focused on her destination. When they stopped at the front, Jake gave her a small smile and winked.

Travis cleared his throat and looked at Mae. "Granny Mae," he said. "Who gives this woman in marriage to this man?"

"I do," Mae said in a clear voice. She lifted Lila's hand and laid it in Jake's. "And gladly."

She kissed Lila's cheek. Lila felt the warmth of it and the small tremor of Mae's mouth. Then Mae stepped back, and Charlie was there at her elbow without making a show of it, walking her to the front pew, settling her in.

Jake's hand closed around hers, strong, steady. Lila stepped up even to him.

"Hi," he said, low.

"Hi, you."

His thumb moved once on the inside of her wrist.

Travis opened the folder. "Friends," he said. "We will keep this one short. Jake is a man of few words and Lila has a phone full of things she still has to handle by Monday morning."

A laugh ran through the front rows. Travis grinned and let it run. Then he didn't.

"What I will say," he said, "is that I have known these two since we were in first grade. I have watched them love each other since. They went apart for a while. They came back. Today is the rest of it."

He looked at Jake. "Jake."

Jake cleared his throat once then looked down at Lila. She held her breath and waited for his vows. "Lila Grace Harper," he said, "I've loved you for as long as I can remember. I'm not going to stand up here and pretend I will get everything right. So here is what I can promise you. I will be steady. When the days are long and the work is hard and your phone won't quit, I will be the quiet place you come home to. I will choose you in the loud moments and the small ones. You are the best thing that ever walked toward me. I am going to spend every day of the rest of my life walking toward you.

"I'm yours. I always was."

Lila didn't think she'd ever heard anything as beautiful as that speech.

Travis looked at her.

"Lila."

"Jake Bradford. I have loved you since I was sixteen. I went away believing I had to choose. I came home and learned I didn't. I promise you Fox Hollow. I promise you the work I love. I promise you that I will always come home to you. I promise you me."

Jake's jaw worked. He held still.

Travis set his hand flat on the leather folder.

"All right," he said. "Rings."

Charlie stepped forward from Jake's side and produced them on a flat palm, Mae's old wedding band reshaped for Lila and a new one for Jake, cut to match. He laid them on the open page of the folder and stepped back.

Travis looked at Jake. "Go on."

Jake picked up the smaller of the two. He took Lila's left hand and slid the ring over her knuckle, slow, like he wanted to remember exactly how it felt the first time.

"With this ring," he said, " I thee wed."

Lila took the other band. She repeated the vows and kept eye contact with Jake as she slid the ring onto his finger.

Travis closed the folder.

"By the power vested in me by the Commonwealth of Kentucky, and by the good sense of everyone in this room," another laugh, softer this time, "I pronounce you husband and wife. Jake. Kiss your wife."

Jake grinned. One arm went around her waist and the other caught her under the shoulders and he dipped her back over his knee. The lace train swept the polished floor. Her hand flew up and caught the back of his neck and his lips covered hers.

He poured himself into the kiss, and her laugh caught somewhere inside it.Every promise he'd just made was in it, and every year he'd spent waiting for her.

Somewhere past the roaring in her ears, the room was on its feet. Whooping. Clapping.

Jake brought her up slow. Steady hand at the small of her back, the other still cradling her shoulders. Her forehead found his.

Her breath came fast and she fanned herself with her free hand, which made the audience laugh and clap some more. Jake turned her and she slipped her arm into his as Travis introduced them as Mr. and Mrs. Bradford.

Jake and Lila walked down the aisle, hand-in-hand, toward the open garage doors and the patio beyond. The sun had come around to the west, and the Kentucky countryside ran out gold past the iron of the railings. The autumn fields were stubble-cut. Somewhere out beyond them was Jake's land, the field corn finished, the last truckloads gone to Waller's mash bill on Tuesday.

The patio was warm under the late-October sun. A bourbon-sweet note drifted on the breeze from somewhere behind the rickhouse.

Jake stopped them on the patio. They could hear Travis giving reception instructions. Lila's heart beat a little faster as she looked into the face of her husband.

Her husband.

He reached up with his other hand and touched the sunflower at the nape of her neck that his kiss had loosened. His fingertips brushed the petals. He set his hand back on her hair, careful, where Mae had pinned it.

Lila put both hands flat against his chest and smiled up at him. "Jake Bradford, you may now kiss your wife. Again."

He didn't hesitate to comply.

Upcoming from Anna Poe

Enjoy this preview from The Mayor's Fake Fiancée!

The bell above the door of the bakery jingled as the last customer of the day slipped out into the humid Monday evening, carrying a white paper bag that smelled of vanilla and warm sugar. Sophie wiped her hands on her flour-dusted apron and let out a long breath.

The oven had gasped its final, expensive death rattle mid-batch of the last muffin run this morning. She didn't know what to do tomorrow. She closed her eyes. She loved baking for this town and didn't want to stop. She was thirty years old, had walked away from a steady (if soul-crushing) pastry chef gig in Orlando for this: four real seasons, a downtown square that still felt like home instead of a theme park, and the stubborn dream of building something that was entirely hers.

Right now, that dream smelled like burnt edges.

She flipped the Open sign to Closed and began closing. She wiped down the counters, slid the last few unsold croissants into the day-old bin for the church shelter, and tried to ignore the numbers.

She was crouched behind the counter, restocking the paper bags she kept on the lower shelf, when the bell above the front door rang.

"We're closed," she called without looking up. The sign was turned. The hours were posted. The espresso machine was off.

"I know," said a voice she hadn't heard in three days.

Sophie's hands went still on the paper bags. She took a deep breath then stood up.

Grayson stood just inside the door, one hand still on the frame, like he wasn't sure he'd been invited all the way in. Which he hadn't. He was wearing a blue button-down rolled to the forearms and dark slacks that looked like they'd started the day pressed and had since lost the argument with August. His tie was gone, pulled off and probably stuffed in a pocket somewhere between his office and her front door. His hair, that impossible salt-and-pepper that had no business looking like that on a man of thirty-five, was disheveled as if he'd run his hands through it.

"Hey," he said.

"Hey."

Sophie picked up her rag and resumed wiping the counter.

"I was in the neighborhood," he said.

"You're always in the neighborhood. You're the mayor. It's your neighborhood."

The corner of his mouth moved. Not quite a smile, but the architectural sketch of one. "Fair."

He stepped the rest of the way inside and let the door swing shut behind him. The bell rang again, smaller on the close. He put his hands in his pockets, then crossed his arms instead, which pulled the rolled sleeves across his forearms. Sophie aggressively did not notice.

"How's the oven?" he asked.

"It's fine," she said.

"I heard it's dead."

"It's resting." She tossed the rag into the bin under the counter with slightly more force than was necessary. "It needs to be replaced. I'm handling it."

He nodded slowly.

He looked around the shop, at the chalkboard menu she hand-lettered every morning, the exposed brick wall she'd spent a weekend scrubbing with a wire brush, the antique hutch she'd converted into a display shelf for the packaged goods. His eyes moved over all of it, noting how each piece was built.

"The place looks great," he said. He meant it.

"Thank you."

More silence. He'd come for a reason.

"Grayson." He looked at her. "You didn't come here to ask about my oven."

Another almost-smile, this one edged with something she couldn't quite read. Nerves, maybe. Curiouser and curiouser, she thought.

"No," he said. "I didn't."

He pulled out one of the café chairs and sat down. "Can you sit for a minute?" he asked.

"I'm working."

"Sophie. Please."

The *please* got her. She pulled out the chair across from him and sat down, keeping the small round table between them like a negotiating buffer. She folded her arms. Her flour-dusted forearms, she realized too late. She hadn't changed out of her work shirt, and there was probably buttercream on her collarbone, and her hair was doing the thing it did after eight hours in a humid kitchen. She hadn't prepared for this. She hadn't prepared for him.

Not that it mattered what she looked like. It didn't.

"I need to ask you something," he said, "and I need you to hear all of it before you respond."

"That's a terrible way to start a question."

"I know."

He leaned forward, forearms on the table. His hands were clasped, his thumbs rotating slowly against each other, the only nerves he let show. His eyes, that pale, clear blue that had always reminded her of winter mornings, held hers with a steadiness that was both grounding and unfair.

"Whitfield's campaign is using his camera-ready wife and they're positioning themselves as the family-values ticket. The stable, settled couple who represents the future of Fox Hollow. His campaign manager, a guy named Rick Slater, has been floating the idea that I'm..." He paused, and she could see him choosing the word. "Unmoored. Single at thirty-five, no family, no roots beyond the name. The narrative is that I'm married to the job and that a man who hasn't built a family can't be trusted to prioritize one."

"That's ridiculous."

"It's effective. There's a difference."

She waited. The thing she was beginning to suspect was taking shape in the silences between his sentences. She didn't want to believe it. If she was wrong, she'd rather be wrong quietly.

He didn't look away. She would give him that.

"I need a fiancée," he said. "For the campaign."

The word landed on the table between them like a stone dropped into still water. The ripple of it moved through her, a flash of something that wasn't anger yet but was headed that way.

"Okay," she said, very carefully.

"I need someone who can stand beside me at events, attend the debates, do the public-facing work of being a couple. Someone who's already part of the town. Someone the community knows and trusts. Someone —"

"Someone who dated you within the last year and could plausibly be dating you again."

He exhaled. "Yes."

She studied his face. "You want to fake an engagement," she said.

"I want to make a business arrangement that benefits both of us."

"A business arrangement."

"You need twenty thousand dollars."

The shift was so sudden, so direct, that it knocked the air out of her. She felt the blood rise to her face. Something hotter than a blush, something that started in her chest and climbed her throat like a vine. He knew, and he'd come here with that knowledge loaded like a round in a chamber, and she hated him for it.

"Don't," she said.

"Sophie —"

"Don't you dare sit in my shop and tell me you know what I need."

"I'm not telling you what you need. I'm telling you what I can offer." His voice hadn't changed. Hadn't risen, hadn't sharpened. "Twenty thousand dollars. I write the check the second you say yes. You buy the oven, you cover the installation, you keep your bakery open through the fall rush. That's the offer."

She snorted. "Like you could just write a check for twenty-thousand dollars."

His brows drew together in a puzzled frown. "Sophie, I could write one for a hundred times that amount and it wouldn't dent my account."

The quiet way he said it—with no posturing, no display, just a plain fact delivered in the same tone he'd use to tell her the time—made something twist behind her ribs. She'd known the Caldwells had money. Everyone in Fox Hollow knew that. But knowing it as town lore and hearing him suggest that *two million dollars* meant nothing without blinking were different things, and the distance between her six thousand in savings and his offhand millions opened up beneath her like a crack in the floor.

"And what's on the table for you?" she asked. "A prop?"

Something moved behind his eyes and disappeared.

"Not a prop," he said. "A partner. For a defined period, with defined terms, entered into freely by two adults who both have something to gain."

"Defined terms," she repeated, and her voice had taken on the flat, incredulous quality that her mother would have recognized as the precursor to a door closing.

"We date publicly starting this week. We're seen together at town events, at the square, at normal everyday things. Coffee, dinner, whatever. We announce an engagement by the second week of September. You attend the campaign events as my fiancée. We show appropriate affection in public. Nothing you're not comfortable with, nothing performative. Just... present. Together."

He was laying it out the way he laid out project plans, sequential, organized, each element following logically from the last. He'd designed the whole thing in full before he ever walked through her door. That was who he was. He didn't come with a problem; he came with a plan.

"And after the election?" she asked, because she needed to hear how this ended. She needed to hear him say it.

"After the election, if you want out, we break up. Quietly. Mutual decision, no drama, the way adults handle things. You keep the money. I don't ask for it back. We go back to whatever we were before."

Whatever we were before. The phrase lodged in her sternum like a splinter. What were they before? Polite acquaintances who made strategic eye contact whenever they shared the same space. Two people who'd had the beginnings of something that became nothing.

And now he wanted to open that door. Not because he'd changed his mind or sorted out whatever they'd been to each other. Because he needed a campaign accessory and she happened to fit.

The anger was fully formed now, bright and clean and righteous, and it felt better than anything she'd felt in weeks because at least it was simple.

"Let me make sure I understand this," she said, and she was proud of how steady her voice was, as though she'd borrowed his register and turned it against him. "You need to win an election. Your opponent has a wife. You don't have a wife. So you looked around your life, did the math, and decided that I am the most cost-effective solution to your image problem. And you came here, to my place of business, at closing time, with a number that you know I can't say no to, and you're calling it a *business arrangement* because that sounds better than what it actually is."

"What is it actually?"

"It's you buying me, Grayson."

The words landed harder than she'd intended. Or maybe exactly as hard. She wasn't sure, and she wasn't going to examine it right now, because right now she was standing. When had she stood up? Her chair had scraped back against the tile with a sound like a gasp. Her hands were on the table. She was looking down at him and he was looking up at her, and his expression hadn't changed but his breathing had. That was the only tell she needed.

He stood slowly. "I didn't come here to insult you," he said quietly.

"And yet."

"I came here because I trust you. That's the truth, Sophie, whether you want it right now or not. I trust you, and I came to you specifically because whatever we might have had, it felt real. I'm not asking you to manufacture something from nothing. I'm asking you to give what was already there a public second act. We have history. People in this town saw us together. They'd believe it."

"They'd believe it because it would look like the truth."

"Yes."

"Except it wouldn't be."

He held her gaze and didn't answer. Which was, in its own way, an answer. One she couldn't think about right now.

"I need you to leave," she said.

He nodded. No argument, no counteroffer, no last-ditch closing statement. He simply nodded and walked to the door. He paused with his hand on the frame. Didn't turn around.

"The offer stands," he said. "No deadline. Whenever you're ready to talk."

The bell rang when he left. She stood behind the table and listened to it swing. A bright, thin sound that faded into the silence of a closed shop, an empty room. And the mechanical hum of the one oven still alive.

She didn't move for a long time.

Books in the Fox Hollow Series:

Sunflowers and Second Chances

Nashville marketing whiz Lila Harper has six weeks, one sunflower field, and a contact list full of favors to call in. The plan is simple: throw a Friday-night concert, save her grandmother Mae's farm from the developers circling it, and be back in the city before the leaves turn. The complication is Jake Bradford — her high school sweetheart, grown now and running the dairy farm across the bottomland, standing exactly where he stood the day she drove away. A heartwarming second-chance romance about family, coming home, and the truth that love grows best where it's planted.

The Mayor's Fake Fiancée

When the mayor of Fox Hollow's reelection campaign hangs on his looking less unmarried, he offers a struggling bakery owner a $20,000 contract for a public engagement that ends Election Night — and finds himself falling for the woman who insisted on it being all in writing.

Fireworks at First Sight

Fourth-grade teacher Wendy Cunningham has spent four years being William's safe place — which doesn't leave much room for a Green Beret on thirty days' leave who recognizes her name and can't stop smiling. But when the Fourth of July fireworks send William into a meltdown and Steve goes dark before dawn, Wendy mistakes nine weeks of Army silence for the rejection she always knew was coming.

Nail Polish and Nails

When the great-aunt she never knew leaves her a falling-down inn, Lyssa Pruitt throws her whole heart at saving it — fresh hospitality degree, no plan, and one stubborn deadline. Tate Dempsey has cared for that inn for thirteen years and resents the dreamy stranger it went to instead. But the woman who left it behind knew exactly what she was doing.

About the Author

Anna Poe writes heartwarming small-town romances that celebrate the power of love overcoming any obstacle. She believes love is the strongest force in any story—and in life—and that happily-ever-afters are worth fighting for.

She lives in Kentucky with her husband and children. When she's not writing, Anna can usually be found savoring the simple pleasures of home: a warm cup of coffee at sunrise, family dinners that stretch long into the evening, and the peaceful certainty that love, like Kentucky itself, has a way of holding on tight and never letting go.

Find her at https://www.annapoe.com

Join Anna's Newsletter

SIGN up for Anna's monthly newsletter! Every newsletter recipient receives a free book and is automatically entered into a monthly giveaway! The real prize is you will never miss updates about upcoming releases, book signings, appearances, or other events.

https://www.annapoe.com/newsletter/